Picturing Lucy

A NOVEL BY
Debra Carttar

INFINITY
PUBLISHING

Copyright © 2010 by Debra Carttar
Cover photo by Alyssa Sutton
Author photo by Leo Arbeznik

ISBN 0-7414-6195-1

Printed in the United States of America

This is a work of fiction. Names, characters, places, and incidents either are the product of the author's imagination or are used fictiously. Any resemblance to actual events or locales or persons, living or dead, is entirely coincidental.

Published November 2010

INFINITY PUBLISHING
1094 New DeHaven Street, Suite 100
West Conshohocken, PA 19428-2713
Toll-free (877) BUY BOOK
Local Phone (610) 941-9999
Fax (610) 941-9959
Info@buybooksontheweb.com
www.buybooksontheweb.com

The counselor flipped the page on the tablet of paper that sat before her and slid it over to Carol with a pen. Carol picked up the pen and held it tentatively and with a look of concern studied Lucy's face. Lucy rubbed her eyes with the saturated tissue trying hard to focus on the pen in Carol's hand. Slowly Carol brought the tip of the pen to the paper and began to carefully carve out the letters in a penmanship that made sure the reader would recognize each letter instantly. Holding the tissue to her cheek, Lucy held her breath and watched each letter as it was formed into the words.

. . . and Lucy began a journey into a life she never pictured.

For Mom and Dad

For the inspiration &
support and for urging
me to get it done.

Love,
Debra

Chapter 1

Lucy was 10 years, 11 months and 9 days old when her dreary life came to a thunderous end. She was sitting uncomfortably at her undersized desk, the one her mom had purchased for her at a second hand store when she was seven, staring at the blank page of her diary unable to construct the smallest of sentences. Got up, went to school, came home played in her head like one of the scratched records her mom occasionally played on the old record player in the den. The needle would jump when it hit the nick in the vinyl and repeat the same few notes of music over and over until someone gave the arm a little push. But no one pushed Lucy's arm, so it hovered over the empty page while her monotonous day repeated itself inside her head.

Her mom was late getting home from work, but that wasn't unusual enough to bring Lucy away from the thoughts of her dull life to wonder about this seemingly inconsequential piece of information. She did, however, often wonder why her long legs provided her with no benefit when it came to jumping or running contests at school but only seemed to get in her own way, why her hair was neither brown nor blonde but a combination that reminded her of sand and mud swirling in a stream or why she was not particularly good at anything. She couldn't draw, she was clumsy at sports, she was sure she wasn't musically inclined although she had never been given the opportunity to try. She didn't stand out in a crowd although she was the tallest girl in her class, a fact that often made her slouch, she couldn't sing (she had recorded herself singing to one of her favorite songs and had quickly erased the evidence) and when she tried to practice dancing in front of a mirror she was always horrified at the result.

The diary was so old fashioned. Why her mom had purchased it for her in the first place, Lucy hadn't a clue. Lucy was sure that no one actually wrote in a diary anymore. A lot of the kids at school had online journals but that wouldn't help her problem. She just didn't *have* anything to write about. At least the diary didn't have a cursor that would blink at her insistently and in her mind bellow write!, write!, write! Lucy was glad that shortly, this diary's days would come to an end and she would no longer be reminded daily of her unremarkable life.

If only she had brothers or sisters, because she thought that would make life more interesting. And she wished she had a father. Lucy was sure a father would give her the resource for all the words she would need to fill her diary. But since she had neither siblings nor a father, she could only imagine the good things they would add to her days, weeks and years. Even a grandparent would be nice. When she listened to other kids talk about visiting grandparents, Lucy would feel like a large piece of her life had been misplaced. She often questioned how she could have no one but a mother. She had a mother who worked and was not there for her when she came home from school. A mother who seemed to try her best to give Lucy things she thought she needed, but grew tired at the end of each day exhausted from her own responsibilities. A mother whose answers to questions about a father and grandparents were neither specific nor reliable as stories often changed just the slightest each time they were told. But the basic facts never changed, Lucy had no one but her mom. And that might not have been that bad had it not added another element to her uninteresting life.

As the blank page of her diary stared up at her, Lucy imagined a world where the small page in front of her would never be large enough for all the wonderful adventures she would experience and all the fascinating characters she would meet. But how would she get to be a part of these adventures? Not in the barely populated town of Elm in the middle of Illinois where she lived with her mom where nothing remotely interesting ever happened. She couldn't catch a late night train and journey along the rails to incredible destinations awaiting her arrival. That sounded so romantic to her. She couldn't make her overly long legs break the school record for the broad jump moving Bobby Jackson to a far second in the category. She couldn't play the piano in the school talent competition and receive a standing ovation, not to mention a scholarship to a famous music school. She couldn't just walk up to the President of the United States and say, "Hi, I'm Lucy, I just wrote a paper about you, and I must say we have a lot in common." No, all she had was *got up, went to school, came home.*

Lucy had been daydreaming for some time, so when she glanced up at the alarm clock on the dresser next to her bed, she was surprised to see that it was now after six and well past the time when her mom should be home. A slight chill caused her arms to break out in goose bumps, but she brushed them vigorously with her hands and they melted into her arms. She bounded down the stairs taking two at a time and peered out the front door before she picked up the phone in the hallway. She dialed her mom's cell phone and waited for the phone to start ringing. When a man picked up, Lucy hung on the phone for a brief second before quickly clicking the off button. Her brain began going through the options searching for an answer. Lucy wondered if she had dialed wrong. Should she try the number again? Was her mom with a man? Why had he picked up her mom's phone? But before she could come to a conclusion, the phone in front of her rang. She could see her mom's cell phone number flash in the screen identifying the caller, but Lucy was too paralyzed to answer it. After the third ring the call switched over to the answering machine and Lucy listened to the deep voice of a male caller.

"I'm trying to reach someone at the home of Marilyn Wright. Hello? Is anyone there?" There was a brief pause before he continued. "If you're there, will you *please* pick up."

Someone else was controlling Lucy's arm when she turned the phone over and pressed the button to accept the call.

"Hello?" she said tentatively into the phone.

"This is . . ." he stopped suddenly before continuing. "Who am I talking to?"

Lucy's first instinct was not to tell him. That is what she had been told by her mom over and over, the stuff about strangers. This man was a stranger but he had her mom's cell phone and he knew her mom's name. Lucy couldn't decide whether that was good or bad. The silence hung in the air as she tried to make herself do the right thing. Finally, when she didn't answer, the man on the phone continued.

"Are you Marilyn Wright's daughter?" he asked.

This time she hesitated only a moment before saying, "Yes."

"Is there anyone else in the house with you? Is your father there?" the man continued.

This man was definitely asking questions she had been told not to answer and she was feeling uneasy and frightened. The thoughts inside her head were beginning to spin. She tried to push the anxious feelings away. When she didn't answer again, the man continued. This time his voice was very soft.

"Please don't be afraid. I'm going to send someone you know over to see you. Can you give me the name of a relative or friend?"

Lucy thought for a moment and decided that someone she knew would be OK. In fact the more she thought about it, that was actually what she needed, at least until her mom came home.

"Carol lives next door," Lucy said.

"Do you have Carol's phone number?" the man asked continuing to talk to her in this kinder voice.

Lucy knew the number by heart. It was one of the numbers her mom had made her memorize. Besides, Carol was her mom's best friend and Lucy liked Carol. Carol was definitely who she needed to help her with this man since her mom wasn't home. She gave the man the phone number.

"Is my mom there?" Lucy asked remembering that he had called on her mom's cell phone. "Can I talk to her?"

"I'll ask Carol to come right over," the man replied. "Please wait right there for her. Will you wait right there for her?"

After Lucy answered that she would, he hung up and Lucy was left holding the receiver in her hand trying to piece together the last few minutes. She tried not to cry but the tears welled up in her eyes and she wiped them away with her sleeve. She didn't know what was happening. Lucy wanted to talk to her mom. She really needed her right now. Lucy placed the phone back in its cradle and walked to the front door and looked out expectant, willing her mom to appear and wave at her signaling that she would be right in. But no one was there. A car drove by in the street in front of the house but kept going. A dog barked somewhere and the wind encouraged colored leaves on the huge oak tree in the yard to dance back and forth like a ballerina perfecting a move. Lucy's mind had gone to a place of her own making. The scene reminded her of the Halloween she had just shared with her mom. They had both dressed up like black cats with pipe cleaner whiskers and long thick black rope for tails. Their ears were fashioned with black velvet and her mom had used more pipe cleaners to bend the ears in unnatural positions. In the darkness of the event it was easy to be crazy with her mom without being seen by anyone who might hold the scene against her at some future time. Lucy was deep in thought when Carol appeared at the door in front of her. Lucy jumped, her breath catching in her throat.

"Lucy, honey, let me in please," Carol called from the other side of the door.

Lucy opened the door and Carol grabbed her and held her tight.

"Oh, honey," Carol whispered trying to control the tears that were now running down her cheeks. "I'm so sorry."

Lucy hung there enveloped in Carol's arms for what could have been seconds, hours or days. How long had it taken for her brain to connect the dots, Lucy wasn't sure, but when she did, the dots broke apart and darted recklessly around the room searching frantically for order. It was the first time Lucy had ever wished for her life to remain dreary.

The man Lucy had talked to on the phone, the one who had her mom's cell phone, was Doctor Glasford. He along with a man in a police uniform met Lucy and Carol at Elm Community Hospital and took them both to see a woman at the hospital who the doctor called a counselor. Lucy felt as if she was a balloon filled with helium being dragged around the halls, and she wished to be let go. The counselor explained to Lucy what had happened to her mom, but only a few of the words entered her brain. The remaining words hung in the air for a moment and then fell silently to the floor. The words she did hear exploded around her. *Mother. Crash. Died upon arrival. Next of kin.* She watched Carol shake her head, but Lucy wasn't sure what question she was answering or if in fact there had been a question. It seemed to be the slightest of moves. Then Lucy heard a voice, but she wasn't sure whose it was say *grandparents* and she looked to see who was talking, but both Carol and the counselor were both sitting silently. Carol turned and looked at her with a look Lucy couldn't interpret.

"Do you have a number where they can be reached?" the counselor asked Carol looking from Lucy back to Carol.

"I don't have a phone number, but I know where they live," Carol replied.

Lucy's head was in motion flitting back and forth, first to Carol, then the counselor and then back again to Carol.

"I'm sorry, honey," Carol finally spoke to Lucy, "I know your mother never told you about your grandparents. It's a long story and there's a good reason. At least Marilyn felt there was a good reason."

Lucy's mind flew into high gear. She had grandparents she didn't even know about. She had grandparents her mom had kept from her. Is that what Carol was saying? She had *grandparents*. Then the realization of her mom no longer being there and the fact that she had grandparents collided in her thoughts and she grasped why this revelation was so important. Lucy's tears began again, running down her stained cheeks. And while Carol held her, she cried for her mom, the only person who had been a part of her life since the day she was born. A mom she relied on to be there every day even if she took that fact for granted. She cried for the fear of being sent to live with people she didn't even know. She wanted to know if they were good grandparents or bad and why they hadn't cared to see her at any time during her whole life. She cried for ever wishing that her life was anything but dull, uninteresting, boring. She cried because she finally had something to write in her diary, but she never wanted to put this dreadful event in writing. Not ever.

"I'll give you whatever information I know," Carol told the counselor. "I would like to take care of Lucy in the meantime, until you can make arrangements with her grandparents."

Carol handed Lucy a tissue from her purse, but Lucy couldn't stop the tears that streaked her face and closed off the air passage in her nose requiring her to open her mouth to breathe.

The counselor flipped the page on the tablet of paper that sat before her and slid it over to Carol with a pen. Carol picked up the pen and held it tentatively and with a look of concern studied Lucy's face. Lucy rubbed her eyes with the saturated tissue trying hard to focus on the pen in Carol's hand. Slowly Carol brought the tip of the pen to the paper and began to carefully carve out the letters in a penmanship that made sure the reader would recognize each letter instantly. Holding the tissue to her cheek, Lucy held her breath and watched each letter as it was formed into the words. MARTY AND ANNA WRIGHT, SPRUCE, ALASKA.

Chapter 2

Marty Wright had just returned home from taking Sam to the vet and saw the blinking red light on his answering machine. It could wait until later, he thought. It was probably someone trying to sell him something or Joe down at the shop asking him about something that he should know the answer to by now. It would be good for Joe to have to make a decision on his own for a change. Joe had been working with Marty for over a year. Surely some of his knowledge had penetrated Joe's head. He was a good kid, but was paralyzed when it came to making a decision. Marty dropped the mail on the counter and opened the back door for Sam who had been standing there waiting for Marty to let him out since they had arrived home. Marty just shrugged his shoulders at Sam knowingly.

"Sorry old pal," Marty apologized. When Marty opened the door for Sam, the cold wind tried its best to enter the warm kitchen, but Marty quickly shut the door behind Sam.

It was early for dinner but Marty had missed lunch so he took a steak out of the refrigerator, placed in on a plate and seasoned it with a variety of spices. He grabbed a drink from the refrigerator, picked up the day's mail and headed to his favorite chair. Since Anna had died more than two years ago, he had slowly brought himself around to a new routine of everyday living. Anna had struggled for a long time with her illness, but still he had been surprised when she died. From that point it was just him and Sam. His daughter had been absent from his life for over eleven years. And although he thought of her often, he had not taken the time to track her down. Surely it would have been easy enough to do. Just find the right person who does this sort of thing for a living. When Anna had died and the whole destructive event with Marilyn was long in the past, he could have put the procedure to find her in motion. After all, it was Anna's and Marilyn's unflagging wills that had spiraled out of control and caused the incident in the first place. He had just stayed on the sidelines like a witness to a car crash too paralyzed to help. He hadn't necessarily agreed with either of them and should have tried to negotiate a truce. But at the time that seemed like trying to convince the early pioneers that the Indians had a right to stay on their own land. When Marilyn walked out the door that day, Marty never believed in his wildest imagination that he would never see his daughter again or the grandchild that she was carrying.

Marty flipped through the mail and finding nothing that was urgent raised his eyes to the wide expanse of glass and to the panorama of Alaska skyline that spread out before him. The Alaska Range appeared in black, gray and white with collisions of red painted there by the setting sun. He had fallen in love with Alaska the moment he had arrived at Fort Wainwright. A year later after his tour in the army had ended, Marty had set down roots making this seeming inhabitable area of the world his home. Where else could you find a moose looking in at you through your front window? Spruce was close enough and far enough from Fairbanks to suit his tastes. He had met Anna shortly after he started teaching English at Spruce Central High. They had both been helping with recovery efforts after the Chena River flood. And although he had known that she was the one the minute he saw her, she had been slow to come to the same conclusion about him. Eventually he had won her over. They had married a year later and immediately had gone to work to start their family. But no matter what they had tried, what specialist they had consulted or what new medical procedure had been performed, nothing happened. Two years later they had quit trying to have a baby. They had been consumed by this one goal and had missed out on every other aspect of life. Marty had felt like he had woken up after years in a coma to find he was no longer himself. He loved Anna, and he wanted to spend the rest of his life with her. He had tried to explain this to her stressing the word *life*. The acceptance was not as immediate with Anna, but she had nodded her head and had told him that she did understand. But looking into her face, Marty had been doubtful she was in agreement. From that point on, they had lived their lives as best as they both knew how. And whether it was some divine intervention, luck of the draw and pure coincident, one year to that day later, Anna had learned she was pregnant, and 9 months and 5 days later Marilyn had been born, pink and chubby, ten fingers and ten toes, and the spitting image of Anna.

These thoughts often seemed to come to the surface to haunt him. But now he pushed the feelings to the furthest point in his memory bank and got up to cook his steak. He let Sam in and filled his bowl.

"A little early today," Marty told Sam. "But I'm sure you won't mind."

The steak was a treat and Marty cooked it to perfection. He made himself a salad and sat down at the cluttered table in the kitchen. He rarely had guests so the table became the surface for a makeshift file stacking system. It would take that uncommon visitor for Marty to move the piles to other areas of the house. Anna would have never let the kitchen table become anything other than what it was meant to be, a gathering place for the family to enjoy meals and time together. Meal time at the kitchen table had been a family tradition until Marilyn became a teenager and then her schedule never seemed to fit the rest of the family's. Anna had tried hard to get Marilyn the teenager to the dinner table with them, but she often became exhausted from the effort.

Sam finished his early feast and headed to his favorite corner for a little after dinner nap. The red brilliance in the sky was now gone and the night had begun its journey across the sky. The store would be open for another hour and Marty had promised Joe that he would be back to close the store. Joe was capable of closing by himself, but since Marty had been gone most of the afternoon, he wanted to check in. Marty left Sam sleeping peacefully in the corner, gathered his coat and headed out the door. The drive to the store was only ten minutes at this time of the afternoon. Most of the students at the nearby University were finished with classes for the day, and with the colder temperatures settling in, were already in their dorm rooms or at one of the local establishments enjoying a diversion from studies. The summer was a slower time for him in the store, but when school was in session, as it was now, his business stayed busy with the needs of students. Marty parked in back of the building and entered the shop through the rear door winding his way around shelving and boxes to the front where Joe was busy with a customer. Joe looked up and acknowledged Marty with a nod while walking with the patron to the register to ring up a purchase.

When Joe was finished, Marty suddenly remembered the blinking light on the phone, "Did you call earlier at the house?"

"No," Joe replied. "It's been busy all afternoon though." Another customer walked in the door and Joe left Marty to see if he could be of help.

When the previous owner of Northern Lights Books had placed the business up for sale five years ago, Marty knew without hesitation that he would purchase it. It had taken some effort to convince Anna that giving up his teaching job for the unknown of running his own business would not affect their lives or their income. Marty was a voracious reader, a teacher of English and contrary to the stacks of material on his kitchen table a fairly organized individual. He succeeded at Northern Lights because he exuded his love of books on everyone who entered the store. His immense literary knowledge made him the go to guy in town for anything related to books. The University had its own bookstore and Fairbanks had its major book chains, but shoppers came to him for more than just a book. Marty had found the same qualities in Joe, a junior at the University majoring in literature. Joe planned to go on to graduate school and eventually teach. In the meantime, Joe needed a job and Marty felt fortunate to have an employee of Joe's caliber. An employee that allowed Marty to leave in the middle of the day to take care of such things as taking Sam to the vet.

A few more customers came into the shop. Marty had a hearty discussion with one regarding the works of Ayn Rand and recommended a book by Cormac McCarthy to another. Then Joe and Marty closed up and walked out the back of the shop together. The sky was now in total darkness, an observable fact that would continue to shrink the daylight hours as the real winter grew nearer. The cold weather had become second nature to Marty a long time ago, but he understood how this area of Alaska was not meant for the majority of human souls.

Anna would snuggle up against him on a frosty night and would say that the cold made Alaskans have warmer hearts. Although he was originally from Kansas, Anna had been born and raised in Fairbanks. Both were an only child. Anna's parents had given birth to her late in their lives and had died 6 months apart when Marilyn was twelve. Marty's parents had died five years ago in a plane crash, and then Anna's death had followed three years later. It had been a brutally hard time for him. But salvation had come from having Anna after his parents' deaths and from the bookstore after Anna's death. Marty drove home with the jazz music of John Coltrane keeping him company.

When he returned home, he noticed the blinking red light still vying for his attention. He hit the play button and opened the refrigerator door looking for something to snack on while the recorder went through the automated message count and the call time before announcing, "You have one message." Marty shut the refrigerator door and walked over to the phone as the voice began.

"I'm looking for Marty and Anna Wright. My name is Doctor Glasford from Elm Community Hospital in Elm, Illinois. I'm trying to reach the parents of Marilyn Wright. Would you please call me back at 319-555-5600."

Chapter 3

Lucy handed the phone back to Carol and tried to process all the assorted events that had become an intricate part of her recent life. Her mom, a person who was always supposed to be there whether Lucy gave thought to it or not, would no longer be the branch that Lucy could grab hold of if she was about to fall. She had a grandfather who was as unexpected to her as finding out she had been selected to sing the national anthem at a school assembly.

At the hospital when Lucy had first heard Carol mentioned she had grandparents, she had imagined both a grandmother and grandfather, but had since learned that only a grandfather existed. She was sure they wouldn't make her live with a stranger who happened to be her grandfather, but soon realized she had limited options for where she would continue her life. When she had asked Carol if she could stay with her, Carol had told her she had *family* like the word family made up for the fact that she was being forced to live with someone she didn't even know. And even though she lived in an unremarkable place, moving to Alaska was as foreign to her as moving to China. It was really cold in Alaska, she was sure of that. Lucy had seen pictures of Alaska when she had learned about the fifty states in school. She was sure that only menacing grizzly bears, icicles as tall as she was and thick blankets of snow were all that thrived in Alaska. It would probably make unexceptional Elm, Illinois, feel like Hollywood, California.

Then her grandfather had called to talk with her. Carol had held her hand over the receiver and had whispered to her, "It's your grandfather." Lucy hadn't wanted to take the phone, but Carol had placed it in her hand and had mouthed, "*Talk to him.*" The first part of their conversation had felt awkward. He had begun by telling her how sorry he was that she had lost her mom, but he had started to choke up and had fallen silent. It had taken Lucy by surprise until she remembered that her mom was this man's daughter and the sadness she felt might be shared by him. She had heard him take a deep breath and clear his throat and then he had started asking questions. She had answered each in one word sentences and another lull had developed over the miles. Finally he had spoken.

When he told her about Alaska, Spruce, his bookstore and about Sam his dog, Lucy had listened surprised to find herself absorbed in the stories. Her grandfather had a nice voice and had told each story as if it were its own adventure. He had phoned her every day after that giving her more details of this place that would become her new home. And now in between bouts of crying, she began imagining her life in this weird and remarkable place called Alaska. She could not, however, image what it would be like to live alone with a grandfather and that still brought fear to her thoughts. He seemed nice and Carol had told her that he had done everything necessary to have her come live with him in Spruce. It was still a mystery to Lucy why her mom had never told her about having a grandfather or why she had never met him. That realization added to her uneasiness, but Carol had brushed it aside when Lucy brought it up.

"Sometimes adults do rash things without logical meaning," Carol had told her. But Lucy didn't understand what she had meant by that.

"Look," Carol had continued. "Having you in his life is new for him too. He doesn't know you either, but you're his granddaughter and that's probably all he needs to know right now."

As the tires touched down on the runway at O'Hare Airport and the whine of the engines slowed, Marty's heart beat began to increase. He could feel his hands become damp and sweat form under the collar of his shirt. He was here to bring his daughter home to be buried and his granddaughter home to live. It had taken him days to make the arrangements for both. Although there were still items on his hastily made list that he hadn't yet accomplished, the most critical had been completed. Joe had been great about taking charge of the store, surprising himself but not Marty, while Marty had spent hours on the phone. He was about to bring home a ten year old, well almost eleven she had told him, girl who would call him Grandpa, although in their many phone conversations she had yet to call him by any name. He picked up his canvas bag from luggage and headed toward the sign announcing transportation services. He boarded a bus which would take him to a rental car and stared out the window as the bus wound its way to its home base. He had a two hour drive to Elm which gave him plenty of time to calm down before knocking on the door that would relinquish a granddaughter to him. He was sure they would be both the shortest and longest two hours of his life.

Marty had talked with Lucy on the phone trying to reassure her as best he could all the while hoping to reassure himself. What did he know about raising an eleven year old girl? Sure he had raised Marilyn, but that was mostly Anna's doing. He did the fatherly things with her like playing games, reading her stories and supporting Anna's decisions. But now he was being asked to be both father and mother. He was older and different than he was when Marilyn was young. He was pretty much set in his ways and used to taking care of just himself and Sam. When he was sure he had convinced himself that he couldn't do it, realization came knocking and he shook the doubts from his head. This was his granddaughter.

The trip to Elm took him along the busy byway through Chicago and then onto secondary highways where finally fields of corn grew more plentiful than buildings. It reminded him of growing up in Kansas although wheat was more predominant there than the corn and beans of Illinois. He grew up in a city and only saw the fields of wheat when his parents packed him in whatever Chevy his dad owned at the time and drove them to the country to see his grandparents. Marty preferred the days with his buddies riding bikes all over the city stopping to investigate the things that boys normally scrutinize, buildings under construction, lakes full of frogs, toys in the window at McMillians, a fixture that years later had sold its remaining stock, closed its ornate wooden doors permanently and joined the rest of the downtown area as a memory in the city's archives. Both of his parents were buried here in a quiet tree lined cemetery next to a baby sister none of them ever got to know. He wondered how they would have felt if he and Anna had died and they would have had to raise Marilyn. The difference was that his parents had spent time with Marilyn as she was growing up. He was getting ready to meet Lucy for the first time. He tried to picture Lucy imagining her as Marilyn looked at that age, blonde hair, short for her age taking after Anna, blue eyes the color of the sea with gold flecks that sparkled in the sun. Again second thoughts filtered through his mind and he desperately brushed them aside. "I have a granddaughter that I might not have ever known," he told himself. "She needs me now." And just maybe, he needed her too.

He took the exit for Elm and found himself passing businesses that had grown there because of the highway. The road curved as it descended into a valley occupied with homes that had seen the lives of many generations. Downtown Elm was three blocks long populated with an equal number of local business and vacant storefronts. At the end of town a modern bridge carried Marty over a fast moving river held in place by steep banks covered with trees. Fall was in full bloom and the leaves on the trees were showing off their auburn colors. He glanced down at the directions he had placed in the seat next to him for reassurance of the street names taking him to his final destination. The houses on this side of town were perfect examples of homes built in the fifties. Streets were lined with trees, from the same generation, that now dominated the scene, causing the homes to shrink into the background. He turned onto Tisdale Street and tried to find house numbers hidden by trees or faded with age. There were no mailboxes on this street, a rare occurrence where the mail was still delivered to boxes hanging on exterior walls or through slots in front doors original to the houses. Marty slowed looking desperately for house numbers as he crept up the street, and there it was. The number stood out like a beacon, a new collection of brass numbers large enough for the most sight challenged to see. He pulled into the driveway and turned the key shutting off the engine.

Then he sat there unable to move as the silence filled in the space around him. Feelings he thought were behind him rushed in and paralyzed his limbs. Out of the corner of his eyes, he saw the front door slowly open and a young girl walk out and pause on the small front porch. His head turned involuntarily and his eyes searched her expectantly. Nothing about her told him that she belonged in any form or manner to him. She was tall with half her body seemingly taken up by long legs. Her brown hair fell past her shoulders and was highlighted with streaks of blonde that shimmered in the late afternoon sun. From this distance Marty recognized none of Marilyn's features. This was not the way his granddaughter looked in any of the pictures he had developed in his mind. He glanced down at the address on the paper he now held in his hands and back at the bold address on the side of the house. They still matched.

Lucy watched him open the car door and step out onto the paved driveway. The two of them locked eyes for a brief minute before Lucy dropped hers to the ground where she was standing. She hadn't planned to walk out to meet her grandfather, but he had not left the car after arriving and Carol had pushed her out the door. They were both watching for his arrival from the living room window, and Carol had gotten impatient when he didn't exit the car. Lucy raised her eyes again and looked at the man. He was tall like she was but she didn't think she looked anything like him. But then again this was an older man and what looks would she have in common with someone old or someone who was a man. He started to walk toward her and she felt her legs preparing to run, but she forced them to stay glued to the concrete beneath her. He reached her quickly, coming to her in big strides smiling the whole way. Then he was standing in front of her and it looked like he was going to hug her. She shifted her body back suddenly in an involuntary movement causing him to reconsider the gesture.

"Lucy," he said raising his voice slightly at the end so it possibly sounded more like a question than a statement of acknowledgement. "I'm Marty. . . I'm your grandfather. You can call me either. Whatever is more comfortable for you."

She thought he looked nervous. She looked at him and nodded her head as if in agreement. Lucy hadn't thought about what she would call this man. She felt calling him Marty felt weird, but calling him Grandfather or Grandpa seemed equally as unnatural. Carol came out on the porch and she and Marty shook hands introducing themselves, saving Lucy from having to make the decision at that moment of what to call him.

"Please come in Marty," Carol said.

Marty knew he was holding a conversation with Carol. He could feel his lips move. But he had no idea what they were talking about. Lucy's eyes were wide and bright and the color of a silver satin evening gown. Her brownish blonde hair was as straight as a yardstick except the ends seemed to want to flip up. Her face was long with cheekbones that would someday rule her looks. And everything else about her was long, long arms, hands and fingers, long neck and long torso and then there were those long legs. Marty was tall, but not the way this girl was put together. And from the way she sat there and awkwardly held herself, Marty sensed she had no idea that she was beautiful or at least would be some day not too far in the future. He realized, while he studied her, that she must look entirely like her father, a man that except for this fascinating child that sat uncomfortably before him was a complete mystery.

"I'm sorry, Carol," Marty apologized. "What did you say?"

Carol had been watching Marty closely and knew his attention was more on Lucy than on their conversation, but she had kept her side of the conversation going because she was afraid that if she quit, the silence would stop him from his visual exploration of Lucy. Lucy had no idea he was doing it. She was sitting uncomfortably on the couch next to her staring out at something which may or may not have existed.

"I thought you would like to take Lucy to dinner," Carol repeated. "I can give you a couple of suggestions."

Marty looked at Lucy who straighten up suddenly, a look of panic in her gray eyes. Then as quickly as it came it seemed to disappear like she resolved whatever had temporarily frightened her. "I'd like that if it's OK with Lucy. Would you like to join us Carol?"

"I have some things I'd like to get done this evening," Carol lied. "But you and Lucy go ahead."

Marty turned to Lucy, "Do you have a favorite place you'd like to go to."

She was going to shake her head no, but realized that she would love a cheeseburger. Carol was a vegetarian, so a hamburger or any meat at all had not been on the menu since she had been staying at Carol's.

"I know a place we can go," Lucy said quietly. "It's called RJ's."

Carol frowned but let it pass. Lucy would be leaving in a few days and she was never going to convince the girl to give up meat in that short period of time. She was her mother's daughter there. The thought of Marilyn made her pause, tears beginning to form in her eyes, but she closed them and begged the tears away.

"Then RJ's it is," Marty said holding a smile for a little longer than normal in another attempt to put Lucy at ease.

He turned to Carol. "I'll bring her back after dinner and then come by in the morning."

Carol didn't need to say anything. They had both already discussed the need to go through Marilyn's things next door. The house was rented, but the contents belonged to Marilyn, well now Lucy. She knew he was staying at the Hampton on the north side of town and that he would be back early in the morning to start the daunting task, seeing for the first time in twelve years pieces of his daughter. So she just smiled and nodded her head in agreement.

RJ's appeared to be a local favorite. It was noisier than he would have liked, but he steered Lucy toward a table away from the jukebox that was crying out *no shoes, no shirt, no problem.* A waitress appeared immediately and took their drink order. Marty open his menu, but then turned to Lucy and asked, "What do you recommend?"

Lucy studied him for a moment as if it was strange for someone to ask her opinion. "I like the cheeseburgers here."

"Then a cheeseburger it is," Marty said, closing his menu without glancing at the pages.

He looked at her and waited for her to look back. When she finally did, he said, "How about I start."

Lucy's head bobbed slightly and she said, "OK."

"I know this is really hard for you. I'm so sorry about your mom." Marty watched a tear form in her eyes. He could see her try to hold the liquid in her eyes but the weight was too much and the tears rolled down her cheeks. She quickly brushed them away with her sleeve.

"I want you to come live with me," Marty continued quickly trying to redirect her thoughts from her mother. "I know we don't know each other very well and that this is scary for you. But you're my granddaughter and mean more to me than you could know. I'm sure you have lots of questions about me and your grandmother and maybe even your mom and I'll try my best to answer them for you in time. But right now, how about we just get to know each other. We'll get you settled. I didn't have a chance to decorate your room yet, but then I thought you might want to pick out things that you like. We can just take it one day at a time and figure this out together, if you're willing to give us a try."

Marty stopped and studied her looking for an encouraging expression on that guarded face of hers. A look that would tell him she was willing to go along with the only plan there was for her.

"I think about this a lot," Lucy started. "I think about my mom all the time. I think about you and Alaska and moving somewhere I know nothing about. I think about leaving the home my mom and I lived in. I think about how I complained about my life and then this happened, like I'm being punished."

Marty was shaking his head, but Lucy went on.

"My mom used to say to me when I was complaining about being bored or disappointed in myself, she'd say, 'Lucy, life is like a drawer. You have to open it up to get anything out of it.' I pretty much just ignored her when she said this, but now I don't want to let her down so I'm going to open the drawer and hope that what I find there is what she was trying to make me understand."

Marty felt his throat tighten and his eyes become heavy with tears he hadn't yet shed for his daughter. "That's what I used to tell your mom when she was your age," he said fighting back a tear.

The following day, Marty and Lucy went next door to the house that Marilyn and Lucy had lived in. Lucy hadn't been back since the night Carol came to take her to the hospital.

Anything Lucy needed, a hairbrush, clothes, shoes, Carol had gone over and had gotten it for her. Carol had asked her about her diary when she saw it open on the little desk, but Lucy had quickly shaken her head *no*. She had made that pact in the hospital and she never again wanted to see that diary.

She watched Marty walk from room to room, stopping to study a group of framed photographs on a table. She tried to be strong, but the tears returned to her eyes involuntarily. Marty came over and hugged her tight and this time she let him because it made her feel safe. When she felt she was done and said so, only then did he let her go.

"I'm not sure what to do," he told her. "Can you tell me what you want to keep?"

Here he was again asking her opinion. But this was much more challenging than asking her what to eat. She wondered how he would get these things to Alaska. Lucy also assumed his house had furniture and the other stuff needed for a home. Her mom's furniture was old both in years of age and in style.

"I don't think I need the furniture, do I?" she asked all of a sudden thinking that for some reason she may need it.

"No, only if you want it," he said.

When she said she didn't, Marty said, "In that case, why don't we clear an area in the living room and you bring everything you want to keep here and then we'll get boxes so we can ship these items to your new home."

It took her most of the morning to bring things to the center of the room while Marty roamed around looking at the life his daughter had been living. Lucy carried things and placed them in the center of the room. He could see some choices were easy while other decisions were made and then discarded causing items to be included in the group one moment and removed the next. He told her to include anything she might possibly want and that she could make the final decision sometime later in Spruce.

After everything was packed, labeled and taken to the post office, Marty called the local charity thrift store and made arrangements for the remaining items to be donated. He settled up with the owner of the house and returned the keys, making an arrangement with her to meet the thrift store truck at the appointed time and paying her a little extra for her helpfulness. He and Lucy had one more day in Elm before they would return together to Spruce. They had spent the last two days together, and although he could still feel her apprehension, all in all those two days had gone remarkably well. At times he felt like he was walking on eggshells with her, while other times their conversations progressed naturally. And now, he was taking her back to Alaska with him. He tried to picture what would happen next, but all he saw was a blank page yet to be written.

Chapter 4

From the moment Lucy came to the realization that she would be moving to Alaska up through the time when the plane landed in Fairbanks, Lucy was sure she would hate the 49th state in the union. The only two things she remembered about Alaska from her fourth grade history class were the harsh winters and bears.

Before her grandfather arrived in Elm, she had looked up Alaska on a world map. Just seeing it there next to the Arctic Circle made her shiver. It was painted different shades of green which surprised her. She assumed it would be white. In her mind she pictured an old time western town with a saloon and dirt streets. What she wasn't expecting was what she was seeing now, tall modern buildings, a wide river running through the city and McDonald's.

The one thing she did have right was the cold. It was only mid November and it felt like January in Illinois. She wondered with some fear what January would be like. Lucy stared out the windows of the Jeep as her grandfather maneuvered along the roads toward Spruce. She had also found Spruce on a map. She thought about it being fairly close to this Fairbanks she had just seen, so even if Spruce had dirt streets, she wasn't too far from civilization. She had no idea how she would get back to Fairbanks from Spruce, but just the thought of it being close eased her mind.

As they drove, her grandfather pointed out buildings and parks and the river. Lucy listened trying to picture her life here. It was hard for her to erase the thoughts she had of Alaska back in Elm and in its place add the scenes that now appeared before her. She would hold final judgment until she reached Spruce which happened quicker than she had anticipated.

He drove her past the University. There were students scurrying about and buildings rising out of the ground like small foothills to the mountains swelling behind them. Lucy like the way the campus looked and felt comforted that so many students had actually chosen to be here.

From the campus he drove down a highway and then got off at an exit identifying their final destination.

"Welcome to Spruce," Marty said smiling.

He drove her down the streets where the businesses announced themselves with quaint signage and ornate lighting.

"Here's my bookstore," he said proudly pointing out his window.

Lucy swung her head around to Marty's side of the car. From the quick look she got she really couldn't tell much. He drove to the end of the block and turned left and then turned again down an alley continuing along the back of the same buildings.

"Come on," he said, "I'll give you a quick tour."

They got out of the Jeep and she wrapped her arms around her as the wind cut through her coat. He took a key out of the grouping on a ring and opened the back door. She walked by shelving which she assumed was a storage room and into the brightly lighted store. She wasn't much of a reader, but there was something about the inside of the store that made her feel warm and at home.

"Joe," Marty said. "I'd like you to meet my granddaughter Lucy."

Joe walked over from behind the counter and held out his hand. She reached for it shyly and shook it.

"It's nice to meet you Lucy," Joe said. "You're tall. I didn't expect you to be so tall."

Lucy was embarrassed and hung her head staring at her shoes.

"Hey, Lucy, I'm sorry," he said. "That was a strange thing to say. I just didn't expect someone who is ten years old to be so wonderfully tall."

"I'm the tallest in my class," she said still looking at her shoes.

Marty felt Lucy's uneasiness and said, "Let me show you around."

He took her down the aisles explaining the book categories to her until he realized that it even sounded boring to him.

"Let's finish the tour of Spruce and get you home," he said.

Home. To Lucy that was a strange word to hear. She had just left her home. Her home was in Elm, Illinois, with her mom and her school. This wasn't her home. Spruce, Alaska, wasn't her home. But the sad reality of it was this would be her home. At least until she was eighteen. Then she could find somewhere warmer and more fascinating than a town in the middle of Alaska. If she was going to have a surprise grandfather why couldn't he have surprised her by living in Florida or Hawaii?

Marty drove on through neighborhoods and areas of businesses down a road that seem to lower into the center of the earth as they drove. When he pulled into a driveway and announced that they had arrived, Lucy stared in disbelief. Her grandfather's home was made of logs. It was one story with a big front porch. The garage was attached to the right side of the house and he pulled up to it stopping the Jeep. She got out and followed him through a door on the side of the house that brought them directly into the kitchen.

Aside from the kitchen table that was piled high with papers and books, the kitchen was neat and orderly. Lucy felt something lick her hand and she jumped and let out a short cry. The dog, surprised by her response, backed away quickly almost slipping on the floor.

"Lucy, this is Sam," Marty said. "Sorry about the surprise introduction, but I think he likes you."

Now Lucy looked over at Sam and walked slowly up to him. Tentatively, she held out her hand and reassuring herself that he was not going to try to bite her, petted him gingerly. Sam nuzzled up to her licking her hand until it was completely wet. Then she laughed and Sam barked his approval.

Marty walked her through the house and Lucy loved everything she saw. He showed her to her room apologizing for the mess.

"Lucy, I'm sorry that the room looks this way with all these boxes," he said. "I've moved the bed over to the side until we can go shopping for furniture and paint and whatever else you would like to make this room yours.

"You have a great view out the back," he added suddenly as if it were a concession prize for living among the clutter of boxes.

Lucy walked to the window and looked out over the expanse of land and to the view of a mountain far off in the distance.

"It's pretty," she said out loud although she had meant it only to herself.

"I'll bring your bags in and then I'll make us some dinner," Marty said. "Your boxes should arrive tomorrow."

Lucy had forgotten about her boxes. Looking around the room, she had no idea where they would put them.

"Make yourself at home," he said. "Then come into the kitchen and we can talk more about getting you settled."

Marty went back out into the Jeep and carried in the suitcases she had brought with her. She found one unused corner of her new room and placed them so she could get in and out of them as she needed things. Then she walked into the bathroom and shut the door. She liked it in here. She wasn't sure why. It was just a feeling she wasn't able to identify. Finally she left and walked into the kitchen.

Marty was busy preparing food for dinner and Sam was busy eating his. The window to the backyard was larger here than in her bedroom and she studied the picture before her. Off in the distance she saw a tree with limbs sprouting out in all direction. Tucked into the branches were the remains of a tree house. Most of it had disappeared with age so that only the floor and parts of two sides remained. She remembered her mom telling her about a house she had once had in a tree, but Lucy never thought it was real. There was something about the way her mom told the story that just seemed imaginary. She had told Lucy that she had always felt at home in that tree house and that there were magical things that happened when she escaped within its walls.

"You're signed up with the local elementary school and your teacher gave me your assignments," Marty said bringing Lucy back to the reality awaiting her and a continuation of panic that seemed to rise up in her often now.

"I'll go over them with you so you'll have a smooth transaction into your class. I'm sure you'll fit in perfectly."

Lucy's fear of meeting her grandfather was nothing compared to the trepidation she felt on the first day of school in Spruce, Alaska. Her grandfather had tried to make the adjustment as easy as possible, meeting with her teacher and getting her caught up as much as possible with the work the class was currently tackling. He used to be a teacher, her grandfather, which surprised her at first, but as he went over the lessons with her, she could see that he must have been the kind of teacher she had always hoped for but had never experienced. But knowing the lessons only accounted for a small portion of her anxiety. It was the unknown agony she was sure she would be forced to endure from the other kids. And to give justice to her fears she had just heard snickering in the back of the room after the teacher had introduced her to the class. She could feel her butt slide down the stiff plastic chair in an attempt to make herself invisible. The teacher glared at the back of the room, a dismayed look running across her face, then turned toward her own desk and told the class to turn to Page 45 in their history books.

By the end of the morning her racing heart had for the most part returned to its natural beat. She was trying hard to listen to the teacher and follow along with the material and didn't realize that the morning session was about to end. When the bell rang for lunch, no amount of cajoling by her inner voice could stop her heart from pounding itself out of her chest. She sat in her chair trying to steady her breath while the other kids hurriedly left the room some giggling with friends while looking in her direction. When she thought she was the last one remaining, she stood up tentatively and began walking slowly toward the door breathing in and out and grasping her chest in case her heart really did intend to exit her body.

"Hi," a healthy voice from behind her said. "Do you want to have lunch with me?"

Lucy turned to see if the voice was talking to her. When she saw that it was, she nodded.

"Follow me," the voice said.

The strong voice belonged to Lily Amaguk. She was so unlike her voice that Lucy wasn't sure at first if this was the person who had asked her the question until she watched her say, follow me. She was a head shorter than Lucy with jet black hair, cut at chin length and parted down the side with sweeping bangs that were locked behind her ear except for a strand that hung over her right eye. She had tried to flick it away when she had said *follow me* but it had immediately fallen back to its previous position. Her eyes were a deep chocolate, her face was wide and her cheeks were rosy for no particular reason that Lucy could tell.

Lily took Lucy through the lunch line with ease and found them a table far from the kids who had chuckled at her with no thought to her feelings.

"Don't mind them," Lily said reading Lucy's mind.

Lucy was waiting for Lily to continue as to why she shouldn't mind them, but Lily gave no further comment on the subject.

"So, what brings you to our fine school," Lily asked closely watching Lucy as she picked at the slice of pizza on her plate.

Lucy wasn't sure how to take Lily, but when she looked back at her, she saw that Lily was being sincere. And she appeared to be waiting for Lucy to answer. So Lucy told her how she had ended up in Spruce and at Spruce Elementary. Lucy was surprised at herself for opening up to Lily. The last few weeks had been painful and Lucy wasn't sure she would ever be ready to talk about it. Lily sat quietly as Lucy told her story.

"I'm sorry about your mom," Lily said. "It must be really hard for you with only a grandfather to take care of you."

"It's not so bad," Lucy heard herself say and was surprised that she might mean it.

"I have grandparents that live near Denali National Park," Lily began after Lucy had finished. "They're my mom's parents. They were genuine hippies, which is why they have me call them Clara and Pete instead of Grandma and Grandpa, and they came to Alaska from California in the sixties. Somebody promised them that Alaska was the holy grail and they nearly froze and starved to death the first year. Most of the group returned to California, but Clara and Pete, this is where I inherited my stubbornness, were determined to make it work. They figured out quickly what they needed to accomplish in the short summers for survival in the unrelenting Alaska winters, which can be darn frigid if you're not used to it."

Lucy sat mesmerized. She wasn't exactly sure what a holy grail was or exactly what being a hippie meant, but she listened completely in awe as Lily chattered on.

"Now they own this adventure travel business and take tourists backpacking through the Park, kayaking, rafting, it's all the rage now, they even conduct dog mushing tours. Maybe we can go together sometime. There are these great rustic cabins and you can stay there overnight and the stars are just brilliant."

Lily was talking a mile a minute and still managing to eat her lunch. Lucy didn't know what to make of this person, but she felt herself getting drawn into the hole of Lily's world like Alice into Wonderland.

"My other grandparents are Nunamiut," Lily continued without a break.

Lucy looked confused.

"Eskimos," Lily answered in reply to Lucy's puzzled expression. "They're my father's parents and that's why my last name is Amaguk, instead of Smith or Jones, it means 'wolf.' I call these grandparents Ana and Ata, that's not their names, it's just what I call them, like Nana and Papa or Grandma and Grandpa. They live with us, me and my mom and dad and two older brothers."

Lucy was still hanging on every word although she was not sure she understood a lot of what Lily was telling her. It was like something you would read in a book, tales that were made up to keep the reader interested in the story so you kept reading and reading to find out what happens.

"My mom stays at home, which really bothers her parents being all about women's rights and all, and my dad is a painter, not a house painter, an artist, and a carver. He also teaches classes at the University. A lot of his works, carvings and paintings, are in local galleries and they sell for big bucks, which is a good thing since we have so many people living in our house.

"My oldest brother, he's much older than me, goes to the University. He's studying to be an engineer. My other brother is a senior in high school, he's into sports and girls mostly. My parents tell him it's a good thing he's good at sports, because it's the only way he'll get into college. He doesn't study too much, just enough to get by and be able to play sports. I think my parents didn't plan to have me, but oops, there I was, so fortunately I was a girl since they already had two boys. They didn't tell me this, but I kind of figured it out. They had to build another bedroom onto their house. Once I asked my mom about it and she just said, 'We called you Lily because you are our flower. When you open up, you bring color to our world.'

"I heard my parent's courtship was pretty explosive when it came to each of their parents. They don't know I hear all this stuff, but I always do. My grandparents were distressed when they found out that my mom and dad were dating, being that they were like oil and water, my grandparents, not my mom and dad. But love always wins out, don't you think?"

Lucy had no idea what she thought. There was just too much information to process in one sitting. She wished she had a pen and paper to write down some of the things that Lily was telling her so she could look them up later. She didn't want Lily to think she was dumb. When she got back to her desk she would jot down as many things as she could remember, dog mushing, Eskimos, Denali National Park, carving.

"Well, anyway, my parents eloped but eventually everyone was good with it, especially after my oldest brother was born. My mom told me a child can cause the uncompromising to bend."

When Lily stopped long enough to finish off her piece of pizza, Lucy tried to recall everything she needed to write down so she could look things up later.

Lucy managed to compile a mental list, and when she returned to her desk, she quickly wrote as many words as she could remember on a sheet of paper. Lucy was pleased with herself that she had remembered them all. But later that afternoon her mind suddenly remembered two more of Lily's peculiar terms and grabbed the sheet of paper from between the pages of her book adding quickly holy grail and hippie.

Chapter 5

Marty and Lucy had buried Marilyn next to Anna and now Marty was standing there watching the granite headstone being set in place. Word of Marilyn's death and Lucy's arrival had traveled fast throughout Marty's closely knit community, and Marty had been overwhelmed by the number of people that had been standing at Marilyn's grave on that heartbreaking day of the funeral. It had been a typical cold and blustery November day, but except for Lucy, those in attendance didn't seem to mind. Marty had watched Lucy shivering and at first had thought her sobbing was causing her to shake, but soon realized that she was freezing in a coat totally unsuitable for the harsh November day. He had mentally reprimanded himself for not making sure she was appropriately dressed.

In the days that followed, so many had offered Marty help, "In any way or fashion," they had said, and he knew they had meant it. He had gotten Lucy enrolled in school and had taken the time to review her school work with her hoping it would help the adjustment of being thrown into this new environment.

Then Marty and Lucy had spent an exciting but trying afternoon at Target while she chose and then re-chose items for her bedroom. Lucy's room had previously been Marilyn's but over time had become the stopping point for items that were no longer used, boxes of Anna's clothing, a carton containing books and mementos of Marilyn's, a television that no longer worked and odds and ends that Marty hadn't been able to throw out. He had at one time planned to convert the room into a home office, moving the stacks of work and files from the kitchen table to some neat and orderly system in this room, but the motivation for it had never developed. His intensions had been to donate Anna's clothing, but the office project had never progressed and the need to remove the boxes seemed predicated on that project. But now he was highly inspired to get the job done and convert the room to one where Lucy would feel at home. The room looked more like a storage unit than a bedroom so it wasn't obvious to Lucy that it had once housed her mom.

He was painting the room a cheery yellow that had taken Lucy days to choose. She watched on with the eye of an inspector letting him know if he had missed a spot. She sat cross legged on the bedroom floor with Sam's head resting comfortably in her lap. Sam seemed to be watching Marty out of the corner of one eye. At one point while Marty was painting, Sam raised his head and barked which caused Marty to stop rolling paint and look over at the portion he had just completed. Sure enough, he had missed a spot.

The bed, desk, chair and dresser she had finally selected in an equally trying venture at a local furniture store had arrived and were now placed to her satisfaction in the room. She had become intrigued with the Alaska sky and arranged the bed so she could sit in bed and view the scenery beyond her window. This fascination had begun the second night after her arrival in Alaska. Marty had heard her scream from the temporary guest room which was now being turned into her room.

"Grandpa!" she cried. "Come quick!"

His heart pounding, Marty had raced to the room.

"Look at the dancing fire in the sky," she had said in disbelief. "What is it? I've never seen anything like it in my life."

Calming himself, Marty had laughed.

"You scared me to death," he had told her. "That's the Aurora Borealis, also known as the Northern Lights."

"That's the name of your bookstore," she had replied looking satisfied with herself that she had solved some question in her mind. "We didn't have Northern Lights in Illinois. "

"It's because of where we're located in the world. Basically it has to do with particles from the sun's solar flares reacting to the Earth's magnetic field," he had said trying to keep the explanation simple enough for her to understand.

She had stayed at the window staring into the sky, expelling sounds of delight like an observer at a 4th of July fireworks display. He had returned to the kitchen totally aware that she had called him Grandpa.

Then an assortment of accouterments purchased from Target was used to dress the bed, cover the window and light the sun splashed room. Lucy set a framed photo of her mom and herself on the dresser that sat adjacent to her bed. And finally she placed on the wooden floor a rag rug full of vibrant colors that Lily had given her as a surprise for your eleventh birthday. She told Lucy that her ana makes many of these rugs, but that this one had been her favorite and her ana had let her take it to Lucy as a gift of friendship.

On her eleventh birthday, Lucy had woken up with a heavy sadness in her chest. Her mom wouldn't be here to celebrate the day with her. Lucy had stayed in bed longer than she normally did staring at the ceiling, not daring to look out the window for fear that something out there might cheer her up and she had been content with the sad feelings. When she had finally rolled herself out of bed and had gotten dressed for school, the weight had become more intense, like gravity had an extra push to it that day. Then her grandfather hadn't said anything about it being her birthday. And it had dawned on her, how could he know?

After most school days, her grandfather picked her up and brought her back to the bookstore where she stayed until he closed up at the end of the day. She would typically study in the back room at a king size desk he had cleared for her to work. A computer had been set up for her homework and a large lamp had been placed on the desk to aid in her studying or to keep her awake, she wasn't sure. It was very bright, casting shadows on every wall in the room.

Lucy hadn't known that on the day of her eleventh birthday, her grandfather had purposefully ignored the fact. When he had asked her why the long face, she had just shrugged. All the way to school he had tried to keep a conversation going, but she had only answered him in short sentences pretending to look out the window at the same things she saw every day on the way to school. She hadn't known that it was breaking his heart and that he had almost told her about the surprise planned for later in the day. Even Lily, Lucy had thought, hadn't known it was her birthday. You couldn't just announce your birthday to unsuspecting individuals, even friends, Lucy had thought.

So when she had returned with her grandfather to the bookstore that afternoon, she had been stunned to see the small group of people yell *surprise*.

"Lucy, I'm sorry about ignoring your birthday this morning," Marty had said. "It seemed like a good idea at the time to surprise you, but then I almost told you when I saw your face this morning. If I hadn't promised Lily to keep it a surprise, I'm sure I wouldn't have been able to keep the secret."

"It's a really nice surprise," Lucy had said smiling at him.

There had also been the prettiest little cake she had ever seen and she had blown out the candles while a chorus of happy birthday echoed around her. That's when Lily had presented her with the colorful rug. She had received a book on Alaska from Joe and her grandfather had presented her with an MP3 player already loaded with three books for her to listen to, *The Adventures of Tom Sawyer, Little House on the Prairie and The Secret Garden.* It had been the first time she had met Lily's mom, Rose, who had picked Lily up from school and had secreting transported her to the bookstore.

Marty had been glad to finally meet this mysterious person called Lily that Lucy talked about in admiration. After meeting and talking with her, well actually just Lily had talked, Marty had understood what all the fuss was about. And meeting her mother on the day of the surprise birthday gathering had put him more at ease with Lucy's constant request to go to Lily's house. Up to that point he had been able to stall or find excuses having nothing to do with why he wasn't comfortable having Lucy visit someone he didn't know. Marty knew the work of Lily's father and admired it greatly, but he had never personally met the man. He knew that very quickly he would have to relent and let her go. She had just come into his life and already she was looking to go.

Now school was out for the Christmas holiday and Lucy was in the bookstore trying to help out. Marty would give her books to place on the shelves, but she would use the time to look up items from the list that she had begun calling, *the Lily List.* Searching through her grandfather's books, she had already read about Denali National Forest, had looked up wood carvings in an art book and had studied a book on Alaska natives where she learned about different groups of Eskimos. She was still having a hard time with holy grail and hippie, and if she wasn't

41

successful with these two unknowns soon, she'd have to ask her grandfather and hope that he didn't think she was naïve.

She loved coming to the store every day after school although she often had a hard time concentrating on her work in the back room on the big desk with the shadows of the light playing on the concrete walls. There were so many other more interesting things to look at. All the deliveries came to this room first and she pestered her grandfather until he opened each one and displayed the contents. Mostly he received books, but sometimes the boxes contained more interesting things that her grandfather also sold in the shop, bookmarks with hypnotic photos of Alaska, magazines on subjects she was not even aware existed and coffee with exotic labels and smells that even she as a non-coffee drinker admired. He always kept a pot of coffee available for shoppers who would take the savory liquid with them as they wandered the aisles. Now with Christmas approaching, the non-book items had increased to include tiny book lights, candies in packaging disguised as books and an assortment of Christmas cards made specifically for people who lived in Alaska, showing Santa on a dog sled or Santa ice fishing or Santa standing outside an igloo.

When her grandfather had asked her what she wanted for Christmas, she told him that she would like a framed print of the Northern Lights for her bedroom. She was fascinated by the changing colors of blues, purples and pinks and then vibrant reds. If her grandfather watched with her, she would describe them and he would say, "I never thought of the colors that way."

Lucy seemed to see things that most people missed or didn't realize they were seeing. On short sightseeing trips with her grandfather, Lucy would describe to him how she saw the scene. A moose was not just a moose. "Look at the way he holds his head up and smells the sky. See his eyes close when he does it so he can concentrate on the scents?" In a forest she might see just one tree. "See that one tree over there. See how its branches all point one way likes it's trying to tell us which direction to go next?" Or in a small village outside of Spruce she would spot an old man sitting outside his home. "Look how his hat covers one eye. Do you think that eye is sleeping while the other keeps watch?"

On Christmas morning, Marty sat in his usual chair drinking his first cup of coffee of the morning while Lucy sat on the floor drinking hot chocolate with mini marshmellows. Sam seemed content with his new rawhide bone looking up occasionally to check whether Marty and Lucy were still sitting there in the silence of the room. Lucy took a sip of her cocoa, pushing the puffy morsels away with her tongue so she didn't swallow them all at once. Both Lucy and her grandfather had slept in longer than usual, but were now sitting quietly each holding on to hot mugs and private thoughts. The tree they had purchased and decorated together sent sparkling light throughout the room. At nine o'clock in the morning, darkness still filled the sky; the sun wouldn't arrive for nearly two hours. The luminous tree in all its glory was the only source of light they needed.

"Are you ready to open your gifts," Marty said finally breaking the silence.

Lucy looked up from her thoughts and tried to give him a half smile, "I miss my mom."

"I know," Marty replied. "Me too."

Lucy opened her gifts. It seemed that everything on her wish list had been granted. When she was nearly finished, she handed Marty a small box wrapped in red and white swirls that looked like a candy cane melting on a hot summer day. He opened the gift and stared at the contents.

"It's the best gift I've ever received," he said letting his hands feel beyond the glass to the picture beneath.

"Joe took it at my birthday party, me and you cutting my cake," she told him although she knew he didn't need the explanation.

Marty picked up the last present under the tree and handed it to her. She tore into the wrapping to find a digital camera buried beneath the festive paper and silver bow.

"I know you asked for a picture of the Northern Lights to hang on your wall, but I think the pictures you see in your head will make far better photographs than anything I can buy for you in a store," he said to her. "Now you can take photos of the way *you* see things."

It was a gift that would set in motion the course for the rest of her life and remind her, years later, that she was always in control of whether her life was unremarkable or extraordinary.

Chapter 6

With Lily as a friend, Lucy didn't mind fifth grade in Spruce, Alaska. Their teacher, Mrs. Campbell, was one of those teachers that made Lucy happy to come to school each day. Every week they moved their desks around into a different configuration.

Once they were in one large circle and Mrs. Campbell stood in the middle turning constantly like the hands on a clock to grab the attention of each student as she talked. This configuration made it hard for her to write on the blackboard. She would have to break through the circle to write on the board causing the kids on that side of the circle to turn around in their seats to see what she had written.

Once they formed stars of five desks each. This worked well for team projects and Mrs. Campbell always seemed to have an unlimited supply of these assignments.

"Here are the new words for the week," she would say. "Each team is to come up with a story using as many of these words as possible."

Some teams worked really well together while others not so much. During the star formation week, Lucy had one of the teams that worked well together and their story had won first place.

This week was the changing doubles week. Mrs. Campbell gave each week its own name. Changing doubles worked like this: the desks were set up in two rows with two desks together in each row.

The person on the left of each double changed desks each half day and the one on the right stayed put. Mrs. Campbell would give assignments and each team of two had to complete the work. Lucy sat in a desk on the right, so she had remained in the same location all week. It was now Thursday afternoon and she was on her eighth partner, a boy named Eric who was about as shy as she was. On Monday afternoon, Lily had been her partner and they had finished their project in record time, waving their hands in the air to be recognized. Wednesday morning Lucy's partner had been Jessica Brown, one of the popular girls who had snickered at Lucy on her first day of school. Jessica kept turning around to talk with a friend and Lucy had struggled to get the assignment done.

Lucy had also noticed that Mrs. Campbell seemed to be gaining weight and Lily had said she had such a pretty face that it probably wouldn't matter. But that afternoon, Mrs. Campbell surprised the class by informing them that she was going to have a baby in July.

"Is it a boy or a girl?" someone yelled from the back of the room.

"It's a girl," Mrs. Campbell said.

"That's good," Jessica said. "Girls are so much better."

"Not if it's like you," came the voice from the back.

Lucy was about to turn around to try to see who belonged to the voice, but Mrs. Campbell called the class back to order.

"Isn't that cool about Mrs. Campbell having a baby?" Lily said after class. "She'll make a great mother. I bet she moves the crib around in the baby's room every week."

"Who said that about the baby not being like Jessica?" Lucy asked.

"Oh, that was Joshua," Lily said. "He's like the James Dean of our class, you know, a rebel without a cause."

Lucy looked at her puzzled.

"You've never seen the movie *Rebel Without A Cause*?" Lily asked.

Lucy shook her head no.

"I watched it with Clara once when I was staying with my grandparents. A guy named James Dean plays this new kid in school who challenges the school bullies. It's actually a pretty sad story. He's kind of cute, Joshua, but probably not someone your grandfather would want you hanging out with."

"He always seems lonely to me," Lucy said.

"Well, if you're trying to compare your type of lonely to his, they're totally different," Lily said. "He's lonely because he wants to be that way."

That night Lucy thought about what Lily had said about there being two types of loneliness. Sometimes she liked to be alone, but she never liked to be lonely. She didn't believe that Joshua liked it either.

On Monday when Lily and Lucy arrived in their classroom, a man they had never seen before was at the front of the class writing a name on the board. The desks were in the same position from Friday which was strange because Mrs. Campbell usually had them arranged in their new formation before the class arrived Monday morning. Lucy and Lily sat down next to each other as the rest of the class filed in looking just as confused.

"Take your seats please," the man said when he noticed the students standing around awkwardly after entering the classroom.

"But we don't know where we're supposed to sit," Jessica said. "Mrs. Campbell tells us when we arrive on Monday."

"Just please take any seat," the man said.

"What do you think is going on?" Lily whispered to Lucy.

But before Lucy could answer, the man started talking.

"My name is Mr. Bennett," he said. "I will be your substitute teacher until your regular teacher returns."

Hands went up throughout the class.

'I'm sorry," he said. "I don't know how long your teacher will be out. Let's open our history books. What page were you on?"

Lucy couldn't concentrate on what Mr. Bennett was reading. She was worried about Mrs. Campbell. Lucy looked over at Lily, but Lily just shrugged her shoulders. When the bell for lunch finally rang, Lucy couldn't get out of class fast enough.

"We have to find out what happened," Lucy said. "How do we find out?"

"Let's walk up to the office and see if we can get the school secretary to tell us."

"Do you know her?"

"My mom knows her from some committee or other."

They walked quickly to the office and caught the school secretary just getting ready to leave her office for lunch.

"Mrs. Millam, I'm Lily Amaguk," she said. "You know my mom, Rose."

"Yes, of course," she said. "How can I help you?"

"Can you tell me, I mean us, why Mrs. Campbell isn't in school today?" Lily asked.

"Lily, Mrs. Campbell had a miscarriage. She lost her baby."

"Oh, no," Lucy said. "Is she alright?"

Mrs. Millam looked at the girls. She knew what a popular teacher Mrs. Campbell was with her students. She wondered if their teacher would be the same person when she did come back to her classroom. She couldn't even imagine how she would have felt if she had lost one of her two babies. Some people eventually get over something like that, others never do.

"She'll be fine," was all she said.

During lunch, Lily and Lucy ate in silence both thinking of the awful thing that had happened to their teacher. Lucy had lost her mother, but she thought about a mother losing her daughter. She wasn't sure if it was harder, but she thought that it probably was.

Mrs. Campbell never returned to class that year. The class finished out the school year with their desks in three standard rows.

Chapter 7

The summer after they completed the fifth grade, Lucy and Lily were inseparable. As soon as school got out, Lucy begged her grandfather to let her go on one of the Denali adventure trips, but it was the first time he had really put his foot down saying, "Lucy you're just too young." She pouted around the house for a few days, but soon found herself wrapped up in more of Lily's magic and her sulking faded.

It was the summer Lucy learned about sex and where babies came from. Lily knew everything. They were at Lucy's house this particular day and the two of them were walking to the far back of her grandfather's property to a small creek that separated his and State owned lands that ran as far as the eye could see. Lucy, who now took her camera with her everywhere she went, was photographing Lily in staged poses they had seen in *Seventeen Magazine*. When they reached the creek, both girls collapsed in laughter.

They quickly removed their shoes and socks and Lily said, "Ready? Go!"

Lucy and Lily dangled their feet in the freezing water for as long as they could before screaming and pulling them out much to the surprise of small fish who had come up to inspect the foreign toes. Lucy took a picture of their feet under the icy water just as the inquisitive fish had appeared next to their toes and just before they yanked their feet out of the glacial steam.

"Does the water ever get warm?" Lucy asked trying to warm her feet by rubbing them vigorously.

"It's a little better in August," Lily explained. "I bet I could keep my feet in for a full minute in August."

Lucy had spent enough time with Lily now that she no longer hid the fact when she didn't understand something Lily said. If Lily rambled on about some subject that Lucy didn't know, Lucy would stop her and ask for an explanation. Lily was so used to it that she would often abruptly quit talking in the middle of a narrative and ask Lucy, "Would you like me to explain that point?"

"I started my period last week for the first time," Lily said as a matter of fact. "My mom and I celebrated with a special lunch at The Garden House."

"I heard my mom talk about having her period," Lucy said a little unsure where the conversation was headed. "But I never really knew what she was talking about, and when I asked her about it, she just said I was too young and she would tell me when I was older. But I guess she died before she thought I was old enough."

"My mom explained it to me when I was in the third grade. She said some mothers just aren't comfortable explaining it to their daughters. But my mom and I have always been able to talk about anything. She says it's special that I'm becoming a woman. That's why she took me to lunch."

Lily paused and neither of them said anything.

"Well, would you like me to explain that point?" Lily finally continued. Lucy smiled.

Lucy just couldn't believe all the things that Lily was telling her. At first Lucy thought she was making it up, but Lily assured her she wasn't.

"When a girl starts to develop into a woman, things happen to her body. She gets boobs."

Lily poked Lucy in between her breasts which had just started swelling away from her chest.

"She gets hair under her arms and down there."

Lucy blushed.

"And she gets her period. That's when blood forms in her uterus and if she's not pregnant it sheds out of her. It happens once a month and you have to wear these pads."

"It sounds gross," Lucy said.

"It's natural. If you didn't have a period, you could never have a baby, which by the way is another thing you have to be careful about when you start getting your period. You can get pregnant if you love a guy and you go all the way with him."

Lucy looked totally bewildered.

"Well, Lily added. "Would you like me to explain *that* point?"

Lucy did, so Lily went on to describe the many fine points of sex, as she put it, to Lucy. When she was finished and Lucy had run out of questions to ask, Lily paused to try out the bitter cold water again. She timed herself and announced to Lucy, "Fifteen seconds that time."

"Oh by the way," Lily said excitedly. "I got my first bra, take a look." Lily lifted her blouse to show Lucy the new addition. "It's called a training bra. But what it's trying to train I have no idea. Your breasts are starting to develop. You should talk to your grandfather about getting one."

The idea of that panicked Lucy. "I can't ask my grandfather to help me get a bra!"

"Do you want my mom to call him and ask if she can help you find a bra?"

Lucy thought for a moment, "I guess that would be OK. It's better than having to ask my grandfather. Do you really think I need one?"

"Oh yeah, you need one."

When Marty hung up the phone after talking with Rose Amaguk, his knees were weak and he had to sit down. He could feel his cheeks burning and was glad that no one was around to see it. Rose had actually handled the conversation very professionally with him, but this would have been hard for any man to handle, least of all a grandfather. With Marilyn, Anna had handled these conversations and he had just stayed out of the way.

The thought of teaching Lucy about sex and the changes in her body *had* crossed his mind, but that would be a problem years from now he had concluded. So he was surprised to discover that passing this information on to Lucy was actually past due. Rose had told him about Lily's sex education class held down at the stream and had apologized for her daughter's boldness. But Rose had assured him that every piece of information that Lily had reported to Lucy was the same facts that she had given to her daughter.

Marty had managed to thank her for the call and for the assistance in purchasing a bra for Lucy.

"Marty, any help you need with Lucy, please don't hesitate to call me," Rose had said. "I can't image how hard it is for you to raise that young girl by yourself. She's a good girl and we care for her. So you always have someone to call if you need a woman's prospective on an issue."

Marty sat there for a while longer while his face began to return to its natural color. So far none of this was exactly how he had picture it.

Chapter 8

Lucy had just passed the note back to Lily who tried her best to stifle a giggle. Their teacher, Mr. Richards, had stopped his lecture and was turning his head in their direction when the window exploded sending fragments of glass deep within the room. Cold air rushed into the space holding the twenty-eight sixth graders and chaos followed close behind. In the briefest moment between the gust of cold air and the confused terror that followed it, Lucy thought she heard the room itself take in a quick breath like oxygen being sucked out of a hole in space. She looked around and saw that Billy Powell had taken the direct impact and was now spread out on the ground, his leg in a most unusual position, blood smeared across his shirt. Behind him Jenny Youngblood struggled with the heavy desk that had fallen on top of her, and in front of where Billy Powell had previously been sitting, Jason Brandt looked dazed, shards of glass protruding from his arm. A row over, desks were overturned and blood droplets made odd patterns on the polished floor like some kind of a secret code.

Lucy heard but didn't see someone slip and fall against the room's furniture as those who were still able to do so ran toward the hallway door. Except for jumping out of her seat, Lucy hadn't moved. She couldn't stop looking at his eyes. They were wide with terror and desperation. Involuntarily she raised the camera she had grabbed from her purse and focused on the fright and hopelessness staring back at her. She clicked the photo and Lily grabbed her arm.

"They need help!" she screamed. "Put down that damn camera!"

The moose was pacing back and forth in the front of the room, looking for a way out. Blood was dripping from its head and it was in full panic mode. Mr. Richards had made his way around the room and was trying to tend to the kids that had been injured while keeping a wary eye on the moose. To Lucy Mr. Richards looked like he was trying to anticipate the moose's next move although everyone in Alaska knew full well a trapped moose would be anything but predictable. Lily had pulled her to the back of the room and was making her way toward Jenny. Jenny was one of the girls that Lily had told her to ignore on the first day of school last year, but that didn't stop Lily from grabbing the edge of the desk and lifting it off of her.

"Can you get up?" Lily asked her.

Jenny nodded her head yes, and Lily helped her stand up. There were small fragments of glass in her left arm and leg, but it appeared she hadn't noticed them yet. Lily aimed her toward the back of the room pointing toward the door and Jenny obeyed without question.

The moose was now trying to make his way back to the broken window but was having a hard time maneuvering around the scattered and overturned desks and chairs. Mr. Richards flailed his arms in the air and yelled at the moose in an attempt to keep him away from Billy and Jason, and the moose returned unhappily to the front of the room banging into the teacher's desk and sending papers flying to the floor. Blood was flowing in a steady stream down Jason's arm and Mr. Richards took off his shirt and wrapped it tightly around the upper portion of the limb avoiding pieces of glass embedded there. With the makeshift tourniquet in place, Jason managed to scoot across the floor backwards using his one good arm and Lily helped him to his feet.

Lucy had remained standing at the back of the room. She still had her camera in her hand and she didn't know why, but she was actually taking photos as the scene erupted around her. Lily glanced back at her after she had helped Jason get to his feet.

"Lucy, what are you doing!" she yelled at her.

The moose stopped as if it had been scolded by the teacher for acting up in class. He stared at Lucy expectantly, Lucy thought, and they both froze in place. The sound of sirens could be heard in the distance, but no one left in the room moved. Almost afraid to breathe, everyone, including the moose, stayed locked in their positions until the sirens announced their arrival to the pandemonium already in progress. Then the moose made a last ditch effort for the window. The hairs on his hump stood up and his ears folded back against his huge head.

Lucy saw the look in the moose's eyes a split second before it took off. She screamed and dropped the camera to the floor. Mr. Richards looked up and fell to the floor purposely covering Billy with his body as best he could without disturbing Billy's awkwardly posed leg. Billy had not moved throughout the whole ordeal, and Lucy could see now that he was either dead or unconscious. The moose kicked and banged its way through the fallen furniture looking frantically at its options for escape. Lucy watched in both fascination and terror. Only Billy and Mr. Richards remained at the site of the moose's entry. Lily had worked her way to the back of the room and was now standing at Lucy's side.

"There's no way it can make it back out that window," Lucy said in alarm.

"Don't be too sure of that," Lily began to say when the moose lunged forward. In slow motion it may have looked like an awkward tap dance as the moose progressed toward the window. Whether it was per luck or whether the moose possessed some genetic talent, the moose danced around Mr. Richards and Billy. It looked like it would miss them until at the last minute one leg slipped on the smooth floor sending the moose's rear leg hard into the back side of Mr. Richards. Mr. Richards let out a groan as air was knocked from his lungs. Now slightly off balance, the moose plunged through the jagged edges of what remained of the window. Both Lucy and Lily turned away when the underside of the moose met the sharp protruding ends of the glass slicing open its belly. Even with all its injuries, the animal didn't stop until it reached the wooded area just beyond the school yard.

Lucy had never felt so sorry for an animal in her whole life, not that she wasn't worried about her classmates, especially Billy. But she felt a connection to the moose. It reminded her of the desperation she had felt the night her mother had died.

She watched the moose as it collapsed under a tree at the edge of the tree line. Then she heard the gun shot ring out.

Lily was still talking to the police officer when Lucy picked her camera up off the floor and walked out of the room, into the hallway and out the front door. The medics were attending to the injured and the police and teachers were trying to bring some order to the group. Parents were beginning to arrive and the first news truck had appeared. She watched parents desperately looking for children and reporters vying for position.

Lucy steered away from the mob and suddenly realized she was freezing. She had walked out without her coat and now the cold March air was beginning to penetrate her thin sweater and slacks. She looked out toward the spot where the moose had gone down, but now the area was covered with police officers and she could no longer see the animal. She was trying to decide whether to go back in and get her coat or stay out with the crowd when she spotted her grandfather running up from an area where cars were parked all over the school lawn. He saw her and ran toward her giving her a hug that lasted longer than Lucy though was necessary but she held on to him for his sake.

"I was so worried about you," he said reluctant to let go of her. "Rose, Lilli's mom, called me at the store. She said her daughter had called her."

"I'm fine really Grandpa," she said. But that just made him hold her tighter. She didn't remember Lily using her cell phone during the mayhem. Since Lucy's grandfather hadn't yet agreed to let her have a cell phone, she hadn't given thought to its role in this incident.

"That does it," he said finally letting her go. "You're getting a cell phone."

Lucy was relieved to hear that Billy had regained consciousness and was now healing at the University Hospital. Mr. Richards had a bruised rib where the moose's leg had struck him and the doctors and nurses at University Hospital had spent the afternoon removing pieces of glass, running stitches through cuts too long to heal by themselves and giving tetanus shots to those who had not been diligent in that regard. School had been postponed for the rest of the week while the janitors removed any trace that the incident had ever happened.

Lucy couldn't shake the look of grief in the moose's eyes. She was sitting at the desk in the back room of the bookstore at her computer staring at the photos she had snapped and downloaded into the computer. She drew a box around one of the moose's eyes, cropped it and enlarged the image. She pulled herself closer to the screen and looked deep into its dark brown eye. She was sure she saw her own reflection there.

Chapter 9

Marty walked into the back room of the store and saw the photos on the monitor. He walked up behind her and she flipped through the shots she had taken aware that he was standing over her shoulder.

"I don't even remember taking most of these," she said. "It was like I was in a trance and my body was being manipulated like a puppet on a string."

"They're very good," he said. "You should send them over to the newspaper. *The Daily Times* always seems to be asking for photos from readers."

Lucy thought about it. Her pictures had only been for herself and she wasn't sure if she wanted to share them, except with her grandfather, sometimes.

Marty could feel her hesitation. "Well, I think it's good work and it shows other people what was really going on in that room. Look how your teacher is protecting those boys. And you captured just how afraid that moose was. He didn't mean to be there."

"Why did they have to kill the moose?" she asked him as he was turning to go back into the store.

"Lucy, I heard them say he was badly hurt, probably when he jumped back out the window. He would have bled to death slowly, and I know it might not seem like it, but it was better to put him down quickly so he didn't suffer."

She couldn't shake that haunting look in the moose's eyes and she was sure it would never leave her. Her teacher had been a hero as far as she was concerned. What he had done for Billy especially, when everyone in the room knew in that split second the moose was going to make a last ditch effort to escape, was very courageous. If she sent these to the newspaper, it was going to be to show the town what a brave person Mr. Richards had been.

She put titles under each photo, found the newspaper's e-mail address and forwarded the pictures along with a note about how courageous Mr. Richards had been and how fearlessly he had helped the students, particularly Billy and Jason.

The next day Lucy spent the whole day in the bookstore with her grandfather. There was no school until Monday and now that she knew everyone would be OK, well except for the poor moose, she was glad to have a few days off to be in the bookstore. The newspaper had actually picked up her photos and they were printed in full color on the front page of the newspaper, her name printed after each caption, *photo courtesy of Lucy Wright*. She felt just a little proud.

Lucy was putting away children's books in the back corner of the shop, when the bell above the front door rang out. She half listened for her grandfather to greet the customer, humming to herself as she slid a book into its correct place on the shelf.

"Are you Marty Wright?" an angry voice filled the air. Lucy stopped humming and turned her ear to the front of the store.

"I'm Marty Wright," he said. "How may I help you?"

"Well, I'm Billy Powell's mother and I want to tell you how horrible I think it is that your granddaughter had the audacity to take photos of my son while he was lying unconscious and bleeding on the floor of their school room! Why wasn't she doing something productive like helping! Her actions show that she must be a very spoiled and selfish child."

Lucy stood frozen wishing the tirade to end when her grandfather cut in.

"Mrs. Powell," he said very slowly and deliberately. "I'm assuming that you are referring to the photos in today's newspaper, so if you had taken the time to look at the photos you would have seen that their teacher, Mr. Richards, was personally tending to your son. He protected him and in doing so was injured himself. My granddaughter did not take those photos out of self-interest I can assure you. And she sent them to the paper in honor of her teacher's efforts on behalf of all the kids in his class. I'm also hopeful that by viewing these photos the authorities might find some way to ensure that something like this does not happen in the future. I'm sorry that your son was injured. I did call the hospital this morning, and I was told that he is doing well and will make a full recovery. Mrs. Powell, both Lucy and I were very happy to hear that your son along with the other children who were injured will be fine. I understand you are upset that your son sustained some bad injuries. I can tell you that I would be distressed if anything happened to Lucy. But your anger is being directed incorrectly."

Marty watched her deflate slightly, not sure if she was going to continue now that he had ended what he had to say to her. He was trying to keep his breathing steady as he studied her. She opened her mouth and them closed it again, turned on her heels and walked out the door.

Lucy still hadn't moved, but she had started to quietly cry.

"Lucy, are you back there," she heard her grandfather say.

When she didn't answer him, she heard his footsteps and tried to find something to wipe away her tears. She ended up using the sleeve of her shirt and had just finished when he rounded the bookshelf and stopped in front of her.

"Do *not* let Mrs. Powell, or anyone else for that matter, stop you from being who you are, from sharing the things you love. She did not have her facts straight before she came into this store. Her actions were only out of fright for her son and had nothing to do with you. She needed someone to blame for her son's injuries and the moose was no longer available for her. You are a very talented young woman and taking photographs has become a piece of who you are. Don't apologize or feel bad about that. Ever. Now come here and give me a hug."

Lucy fell into his arms and the tears started to flow again.

"Don't cry sweetheart," he said not letting her go.

She wanted to tell him that she wasn't crying now because of Mrs. Powell. She was crying because of him. She didn't know what she would do without him.

Chapter 10

Early Friday morning, hours before Lucy and Marty left for the bookstore, the phone rang and Marty wondered who would be calling at 6 a.m. When he hung up, he stood there in shock for a moment and then went to Lucy's room to wake her. Sam followed him sensing that maybe this was something he wanted to take part in.

"Lucy, wake up honey," Marty said, shaking her lightly.

"Grandpa, it's too early," she said rolling over on her side.

"I have a rather big surprise for you," he said grinning to himself. "Then you can go back to sleep for a while."

She groaned and turned over, pushing herself up so her back was leaning against the headboard and tried to clear her eyes. Marty just sat on the side of the bed and smiled at her.

"Well," she finally said just wanting to go back to sleep. "What's so important that it can't wait for thirty minutes?"

"I just got a call from the producers of the *Today Show* in New York. Your moose photos were picked up nationally and Matt Lauer wants to interview you and your teacher on the show next week."

Now she was fully awake.

"I said yes," he said beginning to question making that decision by himself. "But if you don't want to, I guess I can call them back."

"What would I say?" she asked panic beginning to show its ugly face.

"Well, he said they wanted to show your photographs and ask you what happened and probably why you took the photos."

"But I don't know why I took the photos."

"Tell them it's just something that you do, take photographs."

"Can I think about it?" she asked.

"Sure," he said disappointedly.

She caught the regret in his voice.

"You've known for ten minutes more than me," she said trying to give him his hope back. "Just give me a couple minutes to take it all in."

They talked about it for the full thirty minutes, before she told him yes. She remembered how he had stood up for her in front of Mrs. Powell, and she didn't want to let him down. Besides, he would be coming with her and Mr. Richards. Her grandfather told her that he was sure most of the questions would be directed at her teacher and she would just have to sit there and look pretty.

"Grandpa!" she said. "Now you're just being mean."

Mr. Richards and Lucy would miss three additional days of school, but both were too excited to give it much thought. The plane took off on time lifting in stair steps above the early morning darkness of Fairbanks. This was the first time Lucy had been on a plane since the long trip here with her grandfather. So many things in her life had changed and here she was flying to New York City to be interviewed on a nationally televised show, all because she took pictures, all because her grandfather said she had a unique way of seeing things, all because he bought her a camera as a gift. Then thoughts of Mrs.

Powell floated into these recollections. She had never seen hatred spoken so vocally. She tried to concentrate on the words her grandfather had said to her afterwards, but Mrs. Powell still ate at the core of her heart.

The plane stopped in Chicago where they changed planes for the flight that would take them directly into LaGuardia Airport. Both Lucy and Marty were silent as they walked the aisles of O'Hare's terminal to the connecting flight. It felt like a lifetime ago that they had been here. Marty thought of Marilyn and Lucy thought about her mom. Marty didn't mention it to Lucy preferring to not spoil the excitement of the trip, but one look at her face and he knew she too had taken this moment to remember her mother.

They boarded the second flight without incident and Marty was glad the longest leg of their trip was behind them. When finally their flight touched down in New York, Lucy let out an audible sign and Marty laughed. It had been a long day already and they still had to check into their hotel and find a place for dinner.

As they reached the baggage claim area, Lucy was the first to find the man holding up a card with their names printed on it.

"We're Wright and Richards," Marty told him.

"Great, let's get your luggage and then I'll take you to your hotel," the man said. "I'll also be your driver in the morning to take you over to Rockefeller Plaza and the studio."

It started again. Lucy's stomach was in a knot. She just wasn't good at this sort of thing. This should be Lily. Lily would entertain them with her story of the event. They would be glued to her every word as she played out the details with her theatrical poise. Lucy took photos for a reason. They spoke for themselves.

The hotel room for Lucy and her grandfather was a suite containing a common room and two separate bedrooms each with an adjoining bath. Mr. Richards had a room of his own and he told them on the way to dinner that it was very nice as well. Actually he told Lucy and Marty, "Wow!"

It had been 9:30 by the time they had reached the hotel, but by Alaska time it was still early. When they had checked in, Marty had stopped to see the concierge who had made a restaurant recommendation that was walking distance from the hotel. They had quickly washed up and now were on their way down the busy street taking in the sounds and sights. Marty really felt like he was on the other side of the world from Spruce, no mountains, no open space, no animals. Well at least not the kind that he was used to. They found the restaurant exactly where the concierge said it would be and Marty opened the door and followed behind them as they entered the establishment. When the door closed, the sounds and the city disappeared and in its place, Lucy heard murmurs of conversations and saw waiters dashing between tables with the ease of eagles winding through a mountain valley.

Her grandfather made recommendations to her after reviewing the menu and she let him choose for her. She was too wrapped up watching everyone. Everyone seemed so content and happy to linger over food and drinks. She wished she had brought her camera. But her camera was in her hotel room tucked neatly inside her suitcase. There was something alive in the room that she had never noticed in restaurants in Spruce.

Back in the hotel room, Lucy barely remembered eating. She felt she could leave now, fly back home to Alaska, and be perfectly happy with the outcome of the trip. In fact, she might actually be happier. Tomorrow was still there pecking insistently at her head like a yellow-shafted flicker on the old oak tree in the backyard at home.

She tried to sleep, but it seemed to elude her. She tried imaging the questions that would be asked of her and she would try to think how Lily would answer. She yelled at herself in her head for ever agreeing to come here in the first place. "Please just ask Mr. Richards all the questions," she said to herself, clicking her heals together three times like Dorothy trying to go home in *The Wizard of Oz*. She thought she fell asleep a minute before her grandfather woke her up.

By the time Lucy arrived with her grandfather and Mr. Richards at the *Today Show* studio her heart was racing a mile a minute and her head seemed to have developed a fog. They were introduced to tons of people, none of whom she heard or remembered. Her grandfather kept grabbing for her hand, patting it with the other, but it did little to alleviate her nerves. They were taken to a room where a hairdresser and a makeup person did things to them so they would look right on TV. Well, at least that was how Lucy understood it. Then they were placed in a room where they could watch the show as it was happening. Somebody was talking with them again, but the fog just wouldn't lift from her mind. She closed her eyes and tried slowing her breath. When that didn't help, she glanced up at her grandfather in desperation.

"You'll be fine," he said grabbing her shoulder

Lucy looked at him, eyes wide, and thought, "He has no idea."

After a half hour, Lucy turned to her grandfather, "Are they ever going to come get us?"

"Not until the second half hour of the show, sweetie," he said.

She was pretty sure she would never make it.

She tried to think of Alaska and Sam and Lily and home, but her mind kept putting up roadblocks. She tried to image warriors breaking down the walls letting in all the things she loved the best, her grandfather, the bookstore, Lily, her camera. But it was her camera that had gotten her here in the first place. Then she was thinking about the *Today Show* again.

Someone walked in the room.

"We're ready for you," the person said.

Mr. Richards sat next to Mr. Lauer and her grandfather sat at the other end with Lucy in the middle. She watched Mr. Richards answer questions. He looked so composed. Then she heard her name but had no idea if a question had accompanied it. She looked around in panic and then suddenly saw her photos on the screen.

She watched the photos cycle and then heard Mr. Lauer ask, "Lucy, what was going through your mind when you took these photos?"

She had expected him to ask why she took these photos or which photo is your favorite or even how was she able to take so many photos, but in the practice session in her head, she had never asked herself what was going through her mind when she took these photos.

She looked back up at the screen. The first photo she had taken of the trapped moose was displayed there. She studied his eyes again.

"That was the first one I took," she said quietly. "I felt sorry for the moose. He, I found out later it was a he, he looked panicked, desperate like he didn't know how he got there. And then all of a sudden he looked resigned, like there was no way out and he had accepted it. And I needed to capture that feeling he was having. Once I took that first picture, I just couldn't stop. I don't really remember taking the rest of the pictures."

Lucy couldn't believe that all of that came out of her mouth at once.

"All the other kids left the room, why did you stay?" he asked looking directly at her.

"My friend Lily," she said, "She was still in the room. She was helping a girl who had glass in her arm and leg."

Lucy didn't know why she said that. It wasn't quite true. She had stayed in the classroom because the moose just wouldn't let her go. She had been connected to it in some way.

"Lucy, Mr. Richards told us that the moose jumped back out the broken window, but you don't have any pictures of that. Why?"

It was true, she didn't have a picture of that, except in her head. She had dropped her camera when Lily had yelled at her. No, that wasn't right. She had dropped the camera because she saw in the moose's eyes his renewed desire to escape. Someone had screamed and she wondered if it had been her.

"I dropped the camera," was all she said.

She sat at the edge of the little stream behind the house, soaking her feet in the water, which felt warm for some reason. Across the stream, the moose suddenly appeared from the forest and walked up to the far side of the creek. He looked around cautiously but for some reason didn't see her. She held her breath and didn't move. Suddenly the water in the stream turned ice cold, but she couldn't take her feet out and risk scaring the moose. She held there as long as she could, but her toes were turning blue and she needed to get them out of the stream. But just then the moose lifted his head and looked directly at her. For a moment he just stared at her, his eyes reflecting all of those feelings again, fear, panic, acceptance, determination. Then he winked, one eye closed and little wrinkles appeared at his temple. That had seemed strange to her. Then he turned to run and she felt the ground begin the shake.

Lucy woke up with a start as the plane touched down in Fairbanks.

When she returned to school, everyone wanted to know about her trip to New York and the *Today Show*. It was the first time in her life Lucy had felt popular and she liked the feeling.

All evidence of the incident had been removed from the classroom and the new window stood proud and shiny against the winter outside. All of the students had returned to class except for Billy. Lily told her that he would be out another week and then would be returning on crutches.

Mr. Richards asked Lucy to come to the front of the class and talk about her trip. She had been expecting this since Mr. Richards had mentioned it on the plane returning to Fairbanks. At first she told her grandfather that she just couldn't do it if he asked, but he helped her prepare a short presentation, and she now hoped she could make it through without making a fool out of herself.

"Go Lucy!" the rebel without a cause called from the back of the room and the room erupted in laughter.

Lucy was sure her face was turning red. She wanted to turn around and glare at Joshua, but of course she didn't.

"Settle down class," Mr. Richards said.

Lucy reached the front of the class.

"Go ahead when you're ready Lucy," Mr. Richards said.

Lucy cleared her throat.

"Last year for Christmas my grandfather gave me a camera," she said. "I discovered I enjoy taking photographs and began taking my camera with me all the time. When the moose came through the window over there, I started taking pictures because it had just become something that I do. I'm not even sure I remember taking them. That night when I looked at them, I saw how brave Mr. Richards was protecting us all and especially Billy.

"My grandfather suggested I send them, the pictures, to the newspaper because they like getting photos from people in Spruce. He also said that it would show everyone in Spruce what a great job Mr. Richards did and also that it might help in the future for people to come up with an idea so this doesn't happen again. I was actually surprised when I saw the pictures in the paper the next day.

"The producers at the *Today Show* saw the article and pictures and asked me and Mr. Richards to talk about it on the show. I was pretty nervous, but Mr. Richards was great telling them what had happened that day. Then they showed some of my photos and asked me a couple of questions. Everyone was really nice to us."

Her grandfather had told her not to make too big of a deal about their hotel and the dinner in a fancy restaurant. He said that was just for the three of them to remember. She was sure she had forgotten some of the points he told her to mention, but she had made it through OK and was starting to walk back to her chair when Mr. Richards stood up.

"Does anyone have any questions?" he asked the class. "Lucy please stay up at the front. By the way, that was very nice and I thank you for the compliment, but it's what any teacher would do."

Lucy froze in place. She wasn't prepared for questions. She looked over at him with her eyes trying to convey her feeling to him.

"We'll answer questions together," he said. "OK, class."

Hands went up throughout the room. Mr. Richards and Lucy answered questions for a half hour, Mr. Richards taking the lead and then when appropriate, turning it over to Lucy. Lucy returned to her desk and heard Joshua call her name.

"Nice job Lucy, you're a real avant-garde."

She had no idea what that meant or even how to spell it to look it up. But he was starting to bother her. And she didn't know if it was in a bad way or good.

Over the summer her grandfather had actually let her watch *Rebel Without a Cause*. But he insisted that he watch with her and they discussed it afterwards like it was a class assignment. She couldn't believe how old the movie was. Her grandfather told her James Dean was only twenty-four when he died in a car crash. After watching the movie, Lucy felt there was an eerie connection between it and his real life. It haunted her.

She imagined James Dean as Joshua. Or maybe she was imagining Joshua as James Dean. She imaged herself as Natalie Wood, Judy, painfully in love with this rebel. That was dumb, she would never like a boy like Joshua.

Lucy was sitting with Lily on her bed. She fell back against her pillow.

"What do you think of Joshua?" Lucy asked.

"Why, do you like him?" Lily asked, surprise in her voice.

"Of course not, I was just wondering if you knew anything about him."

"He only came to our school about year before you. All I know are stories I hear. They could be true or not."

"What stories?"

"That he was thrown out of the last school he was in and told if he didn't behave himself and get good grades his father would send him to military school."

"Is that true?"

"I already told you. I don't know."

"What other stories?"

"Lucy, why do you want to know things about him if you're not interested?"

"I'm not interested. I just find *him* interesting."

"I think you might have a little rebel in you somewhere Lucy Wright."

"Don't be ridiculous. What other story?"

"He has a crush on some girl, but he's not saying who. Supposedly she's shy, but very pretty. Tall and thin like a model. She's really into photography. And I think she has a crush on him too."

Lily was laughing at herself again.

Lucy turned to her, "Very funny! Stop that!"

Lucy had watched him in class wanting to take his picture. There was something there, in his eyes or his mouth, or the way he stood that needed to be photographed. But she never did. A month later Joshua stopped coming to class. Rumors said he had been sent to a military school in Anchorage.

Chapter 11

As they did each year on Marilyn's birthday, Lucy and Marty brought flowers to her grave. It was the middle of August and Lucy was excited about becoming a teenager in a few short months and starting middle school. Marty couldn't believe that Lucy had been with him now for almost two years. And the thought of her becoming a teenager scared the heck out of him. This age had been a tumultuous time with Marilyn and he could only hope for something different with Lucy.

"Grandpa," she said pausing as if she might not go on. "I want to know who my father is."

Marty sat in silence. He had always wondered when she would ask about her parents or why her mother left and moved many states away from Alaska, but now that she had finally asked him, he felt uneasy about telling her what he knew. Marty himself wasn't sure how or why Marilyn had picked Elm, Illinois, to start her life away from them and Marty had no idea who Lucy's father was. That in itself had been the breaking point between Marilyn and Anna.

"Honey, I don't know who your father is," Marty finally replied.

She turned away from him, "I knew you wouldn't tell me." She was angry at him now.

"It's not that I don't want to tell you," he said. "I honestly don't know.

"I'll tell you what happened and what I do know, but you have to promise that you won't interrupt me until I'm finished. It's the only way I think I can do this. Then I'll try to answer any questions you have."

He had tried practicing this speech in his head so many times, but never felt like he got it right. Maybe it was the story itself that was wrong. When she nodded that she would, he began.

"I fell in love with your grandmother the day I first saw her. She looked just like your mother so you know how beautiful she was. It took her a while to feel the same way about me, but eventually I won her over."

"I'll bet she fell in love with you at first sight as well, but wanted you to prove it," Lucy said, mad at herself for getting angry with him before.

"I thought you promised not to interrupt me," he said.

"Sorry."

"After your grandmother and I married we were eager to start a family, but the harder we tried, the more depressed she got when nothing happened. We had gone to doctors and tried everything they recommended, but still there was no baby. It was tearing us up. Finally we had a long talk and decided that maybe this just wasn't meant to be. She said she agreed, but I don't think she ever believed it. It was just too heavy in her heart. I tried my best to have her look at all the wonderful things we did have, but not having a child really weighed on her differently than me. Yes, I wanted children, but I wanted her more and I missed the way we'd been before. Then a year went by and your grandmother discovered she was pregnant. It was wonderful to see her happy again. And then our perfect baby girl was born.

"Our lives centered on Marilyn. She was the prettiest baby, good natured, and to hear her yell Daddy when I came home just tore at my heart. Marilyn soon discovered she had a mind of her own. As a child it was fun to watch. As a teenager it became a struggle of wills. She was always so sure of herself, not afraid of anything, which both delighted and frightened us. She would take up any mission if she believed in it. She once was arrested for trying to stop a bulldozer from taking down trees to build a shopping center. She was only thirteen at the time, just a little older than you are now.

"She brought stray animals home until she could find new homes for them. If she wanted something, she would find a way to get it. Once when she was about nine or ten she wanted this music album or tape but she had already spent her allowance. She gathered things from her room that she didn't need anymore and had her own sale in the front yard. She stopped when she had enough money to buy what she wanted and put the remaining items back in her room. Anna tried to talk her out of the whole project, but when Marilyn had something in her craw, that's something that *my d*ad used to say, there was no getting her to change her mind.

"But she did well in school and started at the University after graduation from high school. During high school she had a few boyfriends, but nothing that ever turned into a serious relationship. At least that I knew of. I think she just got tired of them and would move on to the next one that drew her interest, although she did have one that seemed pretty steady when she was a senior. Sam, I think his name was Sam. She lived at home the first year she was at the University, but often stayed overnight with friends who were in dorm rooms or apartments on campus. The frequency of that began to increase and we saw less and less of her. When Anna or I would try to talk with her, she would always have some reason why she didn't have time, why she was too busy. Anna tried to push the issue, but I thought, she's eighteen years old, almost nineteen, and I wasn't sure what I could do.

"She had turned nineteen when she came home one night and announced to the two of us that she was pregnant and planned to drop out of school. While I sat there stunned, Anna went crazy, demanding to know who the father was, how she would support this baby, she couldn't drop out of school and every other question or statement I was thinking but was too stunned to ask out loud. It was like watching tug of war with two opponents who were perfectly matched. I felt helpless. The challengers were the two people I loved the most.

"Then Anna said quite calmly at first, 'Tell me who the father is or I will march over to the University and I will ask around until I find out.' Marilyn had replied in a voice that chilled me to the core, 'You will never do that or I will leave this house for good.' Anna said her voice growing louder and more pained, 'I don't understand why you won't tell us who he is. You can get married if you love him and raise this baby as a family.' Marilyn didn't say anything in reply at first but then finally broke the silence, 'I can't Mother, he's already married.'

"None of us said anything after that. I watched Anna cry and tried to comfort her. Marilyn finally got up and left saying she was going back to the University to stay with friends. I really thought we could work it all out, I mean, another baby in the house. It wasn't the most desirable way to have a child, but it was a part of us and would be loved. But Anna was determined to find out who the father was. I'm not sure what she planned to do if she actually found out, but she went to the University and started asking around. When Marilyn found out, she made good on the threat she had made. When we came home from work one day, Marilyn's clothes were gone and there was a note from her on the dresser in her room. I read that note so many times, it's still there in my head like an etched stone that time can't erode."

Marty had paused and Lucy tried to wait patiently but finally said, "What did the note say Grandpa?"

Marty looked at her, "The note said, 'I do love the father of my child, but as I said, he is married. He doesn't know I am pregnant and I will not tell him. He already has a family, and I won't be a part of destroying their lives. I asked you to not interfere, but for whatever reason you chose to do so anyway. So, I'm keeping my promise and I'm leaving. I can give my child a family even if it is not the kind of family that you envision.'"

Lucy sat quietly looking at her mother's gravestone. It seemed such a small thing to tear a family apart, but she guessed that at the time it happened it was more of a mountain than the mole hill it appeared to her on this day.

"I looked for her, asking around, but her friends didn't know or wouldn't say where she had gone," Marty suddenly continued like he had forgotten a part of the story. "Every time I heard someone at the front door or heard the phone ring, I would expect it to be her. But she never came home."

He paused and looked over at the headstone, "Until the day I placed her here."

Chapter 12

Lucy was beginning to call Alaska home. The place took a lot to get used to. First it seemed like it was always cold and dark. She had such a hard time getting used to all the darkness. In the winter, she always felt like she was living inside a cave and would turn on all the lights in the house, much to the chagrin of her grandfather and the electric company. The cold just seem to eat at her bones. She guessed that was why so many people in Alaska were heavy. It had nothing to do with bad eating habits, it was just for survival. She wished she had a little extra fat on her body, at least when it came to January and February. She had once asked Lily why she never seemed to get as cold. "I'm built like an Eskimo with thicker layers," she had said. "You're too tall and skinny, that's your problem."

But Lucy loved the summer and the endless light. She'd go down by the little stream behind the house late in the evenings when her grandfather was asleep and stare up at the bright sunny sky. It was remarkable. The only time it bugged her was when she wanted to sleep late in the morning, but her grandfather had purchased a sleep mask for her of black silk and it became her best friend on those lazy mornings.

She loved the Northern Lights, the ice sculptures at the museum and the ones that were carved each year on the campus at the University. It amazed her how anyone could do that intricate work with chainsaws, a blow torch and chisels. Lucy never got tired of looking at the mountains or taking trips to the hot springs with her grandfather or spending time with Lily at her home and learning about the Nunamiut heritage of her grandparents. She was still anxious to go with Lily on one of the Denali adventure trips, but so far her grandfather had been pretty inflexible about her having to wait until she was old enough.

Her grandfather was teaching her how to cross country ski, which she found to be a lot of work. He would take her on trips to the Museum of the North, to the Animal Research Station in Fairbanks and even tried to teach her to fly fish on the Chena River. After an hour of tangled lines, her grandfather had thought it best if she just sat and watched. Watching him was like watching an orchestra conductor's smooth, fluid movements. The line was like a ballerina fluttering across the stage. He would catch a silvery fish, hold it up proudly for her to see as it wiggled to escape and then release it gently back into the river. Lucy wasn't sure what all the fuss was about, but she always enjoyed the day taking in the sights and smells of Alaska.

Her camera had become an extension of her arms, and she saw interest in things that most people missed. Her cropped photo of the moose's eye still haunted her, but most of her photos gave her pleasure. Her grandfather had picked out several that he especially liked and she had printed and framed them for his last birthday. He had hung them proudly in the bookstore. Now when shoppers asked about them, he told them proudly that they were taken by his granddaughter. On occasion he even received requests to purchase the prints, but he told anyone who asked that they weren't for sale.

Early Saturday morning, the last one before school began on Monday, Lucy took Sam down to the creek to bid farewell to the summer. This was the place she came to let her thoughts mesh into decisions, to think about the past and the future and to wonder about her life. It had become a haven to her and she always missed it terribly when the weather turned cold and she was forced to find solace elsewhere. She laughed as Sam chased minnows that swam along the edge between the mossy rocks and old tree limbs. Looking up at the sky, she watched as a golden eagle appeared, floating effortlessly on a thermal. And as she sat there, as if on cue, the wind began to blow bits of Alaska air swirling around her legs, sending a temporary shiver through her body. Even the wind could tell that winter wasn't far away.

The same night Lucy watched Ana Amaguk skillfully prepare the salmon for the night's dinner while she and Lily played cards at the kitchen table.

"I think I'll be a movie star," Lily announced breaking the silence. Ana Amaguk and Lucy both looked up from what they were doing.

"I'm going to move to Los Angeles and join an independent film crew at first," she continued. "Then I'll be discovered by MGM or Paramount or Big Ending, I just love that name, Big Ending Studios.

"Everyone take your places! Take your places please for the big ending!"

She was laughing at her own joke now. Ana made a clicking noise with her tongue and went back to her work.

"How 'bout you," Lily said laying down a series of cards.

"Seems a long way off," Lucy replied. "We have so much more school. We're not even old enough to work or drive.

According to my grandfather, I'm not even old enough to go with you on a Denali trip with your grandparents. But I like taking pictures, so maybe I could do something with that."

"You could take my picture for a magazine when I'm a famous actor or director," Lily said, excited about the prospect.

"Maybe I'll send the magazines all the pictures I've taken of you in Alaska," Lucy said grinning. "They'd probably pay me handsomely for those."

Lily remembered the clicking sound her grandmother had made and added, "Well, Ana, what do you think I should be?"

"Lily, let your spirits guide you in your journey," Ana Amaguk said.

When Lucy looked at her puzzled, Ana Amaguk continued. "Humans have three spirits. The first one is your future life. The second spirit gives warmth and life to your body and the third spirit represents possible evil and stays with the body after death."

This reminded Lucy of the book *A Christmas Carol* that her grandfather had added to her MP3 player last Christmas. Three spirits, your past, your present and your future.

Lucy loved having dinner with the Amaguk's. With so many people at the dinner table, there was always a conversation to take in. And although she usually never had much to add, they always tried to bring her into the discussions. She preferred to sit and take in the noise, bits of information and the closeness that these dinners brought to her. Ana made traditional dishes, using local foods, and although many sounded strange to Lucy, most she found delicious. This night, salmon pie was served, and Lucy had just taken the last bite from her plate of this delicious concoction. For dessert Lily's ana had made something called Nagoonberry chiffon pie which sounded delicious even though Lucy had no idea what a Nagoonberry tasted like. But she had learned that if Lily's ana made it, most likely it was a culinary delight.

"I was in your grandfather's bookstore today Lucy," Mr. Amaguk said making everyone at the table shift attention to her. "I saw your photography work. You have a very interesting perspective on Alaska."

Lucy wasn't sure if this was a compliment she should be thanking him for or whether he thought her work was strange, and not in a good way.

"You have quite a talent," he added.

Taking this as a positive announcement, she smiled and thanked him. After all he was an artist himself.

"There's an art studio not far from your grandfather's bookstore that teaches art classes -- painting, sculpting, carving and photography," Mr. Amaguk continued. "They accept all ages. Possibly this is something you may be interested in?"

He waited for her reply and when finally she smiled and nodded her head yes, he said, "I'll give you the name and information after dinner. Now, you look like a girl who would appreciate a big piece of Nagoonberry chiffon pie."

Chapter 13

Middle School was nothing like grade school. Classrooms changed for every class. Lucy and Lily went from being the oldest in a school to the youngest. The girls she had learned to ignore in 5th and 6th grades were somehow more obvious now, hanging out in the hall in groups or standing with boyfriends, holding hands and kissing behind open locker doors. No longer did they snicker as she passed by. Now it was like she wasn't even there. She didn't know why, but this bothered her more. Lily continued to be oblivious to them. Lucy tried hard to ignore the scenes she saw every day in the halls but a part of her yearned to be included in this secret club.

The new school was walking distance to the bookstore. Because of the close proximity and the fact that she had just turned thirteen, Lucy had persuaded her grandfather to let her walk to the store after school each day. The trip was in a populated area of town and took her by stores adorned in bright lights hoping to attract window shoppers inside the businesses. It was December and she was bundled in so many layers it took her a full five minutes to disassemble herself from her outerwear once she reached the bookstore. With Christmas shopping in full swing, the store windows along her path were adorned with Christmas lights and gifts that were used to lure customers inside.

Lucy was taking a side trip this afternoon. She had calculated that it would only take ten extra minutes and she was sure her grandfather wouldn't notice if she arrived a few minutes later than usual. It appeared to Lucy that he gave her an extra fifteen minutes before he started to panic, so she was hopeful she would make it before this deadline. She had run out of school and the first five blocks to give herself added time, and now she was standing in front of the glass door cupping her hand over the surface to see inside more clearly. Suddenly the door pulled open and she nearly fell to the floor inside the studio.

"Welcome to Webber-Ellis Art Studio," a man said helping her regain her balance by grabbing her elbow. Lucy's eyes traveled around the room taking in the colors, shapes and designs.

"Are you interested in a class?" the man asked. "How about a tour?"

"Yes," Lucy replied. "And yes."

He explained to her how the studio was named after two European explorers who drew and sketched pictures to record what the travelers were encountering in Alaska.

"It was their version of the camera at the time which was in the late 1700's," he said. "This room over here is used to teach carving including the tradition of totem pole motifs. The front area you saw when you came in is where we hold painting, drawing and sketching classes and over there is a lecture room and photography studio.

"I'm remiss," he said suddenly. "My name is Michael Service. And you are?"

"Lucy," she said, "Lucy Wright."

"Well Lucy Wright," Michael said. "How may I be of service?"

He smiled at his play on words and Lucy gave a little laugh.

"I might be interested in photography classes," she said, a serious expression replacing the smile.

"Follow me to the counter and I'll give you a brochure on the classes we offer," Michael said directing her to a small area in the front of the studio.

On her way to the bookstore, she studied the classes and was shocked at the cost of each session. She could ask her grandfather, but he already gave her so much. Her unexpected appearance into his life must be costing him money he hadn't anticipated spending, although he'd never said anything about it to her. She just couldn't ask him for this. She reached the door to the bookstore and went inside. He was at the front counter ringing up a purchase, but raised his head and waved at her. Lucy smiled at him but kept on going to the back room. Once there she starting removing the layers of clothing that had kept her warm outdoors, hanging each piece on the hooks her grandfather had provided for her. She sat down at the desk and tried to study, but the thoughts of the art studio kept intercepting her thoughts of school work, so she walked back into the store and aimlessly walked the aisles of books. She stopped occasionally and studied the titles, pulling a book out randomly to look at the cover. She followed the row of books to the front of the store pausing to look at the holiday items displayed for sale. Her grandfather had finished with the customer and was approaching her.

"What happened at school today?" he asked.

He asked her the same questions every day, so she always tried to prepare herself with some small tidbit of information she could share with him. When he first began asking her this question, she would answer "nothing." But he would talk with her until he discovered some small morsel of news she had forgotten about. After going through this routine several times in a row, she had finally understood what he was doing and began examining each day herself to find that piece of interesting information she could pass on to him.

"Lily's trying out for the school play, *Wizard of Oz*," Lucy told him.

"Does she want to be Dorothy?" he asked.

"Lily? No way," she said. "She wants to be Glinda, the good witch. Something about the dress."

They were both laughing when another customer came into the shop and Marty left to offer help. Lucy was left standing there holding a coffee table book on different Christmas traditions she had picked up from a table. She thumbed through the pages examining each photograph identifying how she would have changed each one, a different angle, different lighting, different coloring. She placed the book back on the table exactly where it had been and let her eyes wander around the store. She liked being here. There was both an energy and a quietness that suited her. She stopped when her eyes reached her framed photographs hung on the wall behind the counter. She stared at them and let an idea form in her head until a smile formed on her lips. She knew how she could pay for the photography classes at the art studio. Now she had to convince her grandfather.

Lucy spent the following days working on the details of her idea before she presented it to her grandfather. She found herself daydreaming in class. When a teacher had caught her staring out the window and had called her name, she had looked at him puzzled having no idea what response he expected from her. The class had responded with giggles until the teacher brought the room back to order. Now she forced herself to concentrate on her school work. Winter break was just around the corner, so she'd have plenty of time to put the information together when school wouldn't get in the way. The next photography class didn't begin until mid January. She would work things out by the end of December.

She was busy at her locker, putting away her math book and getting out her science book when she heard Lily yell her name. Lucy looked up and saw Lily walking at a fast pace toward her. Lucy could tell she wanted to run, but Lily had already received one warning for running in the hallways, so now she was speed walking through the crowd of students.

"Lucy, I got the part," she said out of breath from her trek down the aisle. "I got the part of Glinda!"

"They took one look at me and asked me if I wanted to try out to be a munchkin. But I said, 'Why do you want me to be a munchkin? I want the part of Glinda.' I heard them whispering between themselves. They were sitting in the auditorium seats and I couldn't see them because the spotlight was shining on the stage and basically blinding me. I was just standing there waiting for them and finally couldn't wait any longer so in a powerful but sweet loving voice I began reciting the line about the silver shoes and their power to take its wearer anywhere by wishing and clicking the heals." Lily was waving her arm about as if she was directing a band with a magic wand.

"I heard one of them say, 'We can make the gown longer and have her stand on a crate.' Finally someone said, 'Fine, thank you Lily, the parts will be chosen and displayed on the main announcement board on Friday.' Lucy, the list just went up and my name was there, right next to the name of Glinda!"

"I thought it was a pair of ruby slippers?" Lucy asked.

"That's the movie version," Lily corrected her. "In the book, the slippers are silver just like my flowing gown will be."

She was twirling herself down the hall now as Lucy shut her locker door.

"Saturday!" Lily called out stopping to click her heels three times.

"'You are unusual," Lucy said to herself.

Lucy's grandfather had dropped her off at Lily's on his way to open the bookstore. They were sitting on Lily's bed and Lily was talking her usual mile a minute.

"I think I'm in love," she said batting her eyes and then pretending to faint on the bed. "His name is Tommy Birdsall." He's playing the part of the cowardly lion. And I hope he has the *courage* to talk to me."

Lily laughed so hard she rolled off the bed and was now sprawled across the bedroom floor.

"He's in eighth grade," she continued from her position on the floor. "And he's beyond handsome."

"I haven't talked with you all week," Lily said suddenly changing the subject as Lily so often did. "What's new with you, *my pretty?"*

She laughed at herself again.

"Will you please get off the floor," Lucy said. "I've been working up this idea and I want to see what you think."

To Lucy's surprise, Lily listened without interrupting.

"I'm nervous about asking my grandfather," Lucy said when she was finished.

Lily grabbed her by the shoulders and looked directly into Lucy's eyes. In a deep and powerful voice she became the cowardly lion trying to convince himself of his bravery. "What makes a mother protect her child? Courage! What makes a plant rise out of the ground? Courage! What makes the wind dance with a tree? Courage!"

Lucy had worked the details out in her head so many times that she felt she was also memorizing lines for a play. It was a week before Christmas, and she had finally worked up the courage to talk with her grandfather about her idea. She had been studying in her room and now walked out to find him reading in his favorite chair.

"Can I talk to you a minute?" she asked, taking a seat on the couch across from him.

He set the book aside and gave her his full attention. She took in a deep breath, held it there for a moment and expelled the air creating a void in her lungs. She had to take another breath to start talking.

"There's this art studio not far from the bookstore," she began. "Lily's dad first told me about it. They have classes in photography along with other types of art instruction. And I was thinking I would like to take a class there beginning in January. The photography class that I would take is on Saturday mornings, so it wouldn't get in the way of school."

She breathed in and out again. Marty was studying her, but remained quiet and watched her catch her breath before continuing.

"Here's a brochure. The classes are kind of expensive. So I had an idea that would let me pay for the classes. Remember you said that some customers had inquired about purchasing the photographs in the bookstore. Well, I can print more of the really good ones, frame them and put them up for sale in the bookstore. I would have some expenses, like the frames and the printing costs. I did a little research and I think they should be 9 X 13 with a matte, but I don't have a printer that will print that size. Yet. Anyway, maybe I can borrow the money for frames and printing and then pay you back as pictures sell. I'd really like to start the January class, but I can wait if I don't have enough money in time."

She paused and then said, "That's it."

"You have obviously given this much thought," he said. "Basically I think it's a good idea, but give me a day or two to digest it all. Can you do that?"

She was heartbroken but said, "Yes."

"I'm really happy that you've found something you love," he said when he saw the dejection appear across her face. "I'm really proud of you."

He smiled at her and she tried her best to smile back. The wait was going to be unbearable.

Marty had read through the brochure for the art studio and was impressed at the classes it offered. The next afternoon when Joe arrived at the store, he left the shop and walked to the art studio on Mission Street. He walked inside and a young man greeted him.

"How can I help you?" the young man said.

"I'm here inquiring about classes for my granddaughter and I wanted to take a look at the facilities," Marty answered.

"Well, my name is Michael Service. Let me show you around."

"Marty Wright," Marty said taking Michael's hand and shaking it firmly. "I'm inquiring for my granddaughter Lucy."

"Lucy Wright?" Michael said with a question. "I met a Lucy Wright. She was interested in photography classes."

"My granddaughter was here?" Marty asked surprised that Lucy had been here. She hadn't mentioned that part.

"Well," Michael said trying to reassure the man that his granddaughter hadn't done something daring without his knowledge. "I don't think she planned to come in, but I opened the door as she was peering in and she kind of just fell inside. I'll give you the tour I gave to her. Follow me."

When the tour concluded, Marty asked Michael a number of questions about the studio, photography classes and about equipment. It turned out that Michael had graduated from the University with an art degree and ran the studio with his partner, a local artist that Marty remembered reading about in some publication. Michael went through the different photography classes describing what was taught in each and explained to Marty camera equipment that Lucy would need to do her work and what was provided by the studio.

"How did Lucy hear about us?" Michael asked.

"Her friend's father, Ben Amaguk, suggested your studio to her," Marty replied.

"I'm impressed!" Michael said astonished at the connection. "He's an awesome artist. I actually took one of his classes at the University."

"I'd like to sign Lucy up for the class you suggested that starts in January," Marty told him. "I can just picture her face when she finds out she's enrolled in the class."

Chapter 14

It had been three days since Lucy had confronted her grandfather with the idea to raise money for photography classes. That afternoon when she arrived at the store, she greeted her grandfather with an expectant smile, never noticing that her framed photographs no longer hung on the wall. Joe was there helping a customer, and she gave him a small wave before heading to the back room. She sat down at the desk without shedding her layers of outerwear. She couldn't take this anymore. She wondered when her grandfather was going to tell her whether he would help her with her idea. Maybe he would say she was too young to take photography classes. It seemed like he felt she was too young for everything else. She was talking herself into a disheartened state, when her grandfather walked into the back room.

"What happened at school today?" he asked.

She really wanted to say nothing. She wondered whether he had forgotten about their previous conversation.

"I think I forgot to tell you that Lily got the part of Glinda in *The Wizard of Oz,*" she said not putting much enthusiasm into the answer.

He watched her closely and then reached for a folding chair that was leaning against the wall, opened it and set it in front of her.

"I stopped into the art studio today," he said causing Lucy to look up surprised.

"I talked to a very nice young man named Michael Service," her grandfather added.

Lucy was looking at him with panic in her eyes now.

"Image how surprised I was when he told me that he had already met you," he said watching her squirm.

Suddenly Lucy felt really hot under all those layers and she was sorry she hadn't taken the time to remove them.

"I talked to him for some time," Marty said slowly. "He suggested you start with the basic digital photography class."

He paused and Lucy felt the seconds tick away in double time as they matched the rapid beat of her heart.

Finally he continued, "So I signed you up for the class that starts January 15."

The ticking clock stopped and she jumped out of the chair and hugged him.

"Thank you Grandpa!" she cried.

Then she added, "But I want to pay for the classes myself."

"I've been giving your idea a lot of thought and I think with some fine tuning it's a great plan," Marty said. "First thing you have to do is print me more photos to go on my wall in the store. I wanted to test the market, not really wanting to sell those wonderful photographs from you, and ended up selling all four of them."

Lucy didn't know what to say. She was having a hard time believing that someone actually wanted to buy her photographs.

"I priced them at $85 each," he continued.

Lucy's mouth dropped. She had printed them herself and had purchased ready-made frames with mats that she had found on sale for $15 each. She had used all of her saved allowance on the four prints.

But before she could say anything, Marty continued, "But I think I have an idea to ask for a little more. If you limit the number of each photo that you print, number the prints and sign and date the photos in the bottom corner, I would suggest we put a price of $125 on each."

Lucy couldn't speak. Nowhere in her planning had she thought about getting this much money for her photographs.

"So, Lucy," her grandfather said. "Those four photographs already paid for your first class, plus you have some additional funds to pay for materials you'll need if you really want to pay for this yourself. Mr. Service gave me a list of the things you'll need."

"Thank you, Grandpa," she said smiling so hard it almost hurt. "Yes, I want to pay. Thank you for everything."

"Now your school work can't suffer," he said. "Or we'll have to re-evaluate this whole enterprise. You'll have two weeks off for winter break. That'll give you a good head start on filling the shop walls with your photographs."

As soon as Marty went back up front, Lucy called Lily and gave her the news. Even through the closed door, Marty could hear her screams of delight. Now he couldn't wait until Christmas morning.

When Lucy got up on Christmas morning, Marty and Sam were already waiting for her.

"Merry Christmas," Marty said to her.

"Merry Christmas," she replied still a bit groggy.

She shuffled into the kitchen to make herself a cup of hot chocolate and Sam followed her, his tail wagging purposefully, as if begging her to hurry up. The microwave dinged and she carefully removed the cup of hot water, added the chocolate mix and stirred the powder until the mini marshmallows raced in a circle in the middle of the cup. She carried the steaming cup back to the couch and sat down carefully eyeing her grandfather. Something was up, she thought.

She blew on her hot chocolate and then set the cup down on the table next to her. Rising from the couch she went to the tree and studied the decorations that hung there. Sam stood up expectantly and Lucy knelt down and picked up a gift from under the tree. She opened the box, took out the rawhide bone she had previously placed inside and handed it to Sam.

"Merry Christmas, Sam," she said patting him on the head.

He took the bone, spread himself out on the floor and began working on the knot.

Lucy knelt down again and took a wrapped parcel from under the tree and held it up as if checking to see whose name was written there.

"It's for you Grandpa," she said. "I wonder what it could be?"

They liked playing this game each Christmas. It was the gift she had spent hours working on for him and she knew perfectly well what it was.

He accepted the package from her and pretended to rattle it and then began removing the paper adorned in silver bells.

"Plug it in Grandpa," she said not waiting for him to finish taking it out of the box.

He reached over and plugged it into the wall socket. A photo appeared, then faded and another emerged. They were of him and Lucy and Alaska.

"It's using a memory card and I can update it for you," Lucy said.

"It's perfect Lucy," Marty said.

He got up from his chair and gave her a hug. Then Lucy devoured the remaining gifts under the tree. When the last gift was opened and inspected, Lucy sat back down on the couch exhausted.

"I think you missed a gift," Marty said. "Over there by the table."

She followed his gaze and then walked over and picked up the gift. She gave it a little shake and then began opening the present.

"Oh, Grandpa," she screamed in delight. "This is so expensive."

"I just thought you should have a professional camera for your classes," her grandfather added. "Michael Service recommended that digital single-lens reflex model."

She ran over to him and gave him a hug.

"Thank you, thank you, thank you," she said dancing in a circle.

Sam looked up at the commotion but seeing nothing of interest to him went back to working on the bone.

Lucy spent the Christmas holidays reading her camera's manual, trying out the different settings and features and choosing photographs to print, matte and frame. With her grandfather's help, they chose ten different prints to sell. He helped her set up a system so she would know how many of each she had printed and what number she was on. He also showed her how to keep track of her income and expenses. They had the photos printed at a local print shop, found premade frames and had mats custom made for the finishing touch. Lucy decided to place each photo off center in the frame giving the prints a more distinctive appearance. Before placing the photographs in the frames, Lucy signed, numbered and dated each photo carefully. Then Marty took them to the bookstore and hung them on the wall. It was after Christmas now and in the heart of the cold winter, so Marty prepared her that sales of her photos might be slow.

"As soon as I pay you back for the expenses so far," Lucy said, "I'd like to buy a printer so I can print the photographs myself. I've studied the printers that can print this size, and they're all pretty expensive, so it will take me some time to save up."

"Let's not get ahead of ourselves," Marty said. "Let's take it one day at a time and see what develops."

Lucy rolled her eyes at her grandfather.

"Funny, Grandpa," she said. "Hilarious."

They hung the photos, but after a week all ten still hung on the wall at the bookshop. School was back in session and Lucy was getting excited about her first day of class at the art studio and tried not to think about the unsold photos. Lily's theatre group started rehearsing for the play and the two girls began to see less of each other. Just the other day Lucy had spied Lily walking down the hall with a boy. Lily had waved at her but hadn't stopped to talk. Lucy wondered if this was Tommy Birdsall, the cowardly lion. He hadn't looked so cowardly walking down the hall with Lily. Lucy had watched him slip his hand into Lily's. What surprised her more is that Lily had accepted it, intertwining her fingers in his. A pang of jealously had ripped through Lucy's body at the time. Now she tried not to think about it, instead making plans in her mind to call Lily on Saturday.

But Lucy soon found out that on Saturdays the whole production of *The Wizard of Oz* would be meeting for rehearsals. Lucy's photography class began in a week so neither of them would be available on Saturdays for a while. Lucy asked Lily about Sunday afternoon, but Lily said she was practicing her lines with some of the cast and would try to get together with her the following Sunday.

Lucy pouted around the bookstore each afternoon. When Marty couldn't take it anymore, he took her to the back room and sat her down at the desk.

"Spill," he said. "You've been moping around here for a week. I thought you'd be excited about your class, your photographs and your new camera. But obviously something is bothering you. So spill."

She told him about Lily and never getting to see her anymore. She told him the play was taking up all of Lily's time and she said Lily couldn't seem to find time for her anymore. She left out the part about the boy. She had a feeling that her grandfather would think they were too young to be holding hands with a boy. And she didn't want him to question her being able to see Lily. That is if they ever did see each other again. Finally she stopped talking and groaned.

"Lucy," Marty started. "You and Lily have been best friends for two years. Both you and Lily will have many friends over your lifetimes. But a friendship like the two of you have will always be special whether you are joined at the hips or whether time takes you down different paths. She was there for you when you were new to Alaska and new to the fifth grade. She has always been happy for you whether it was sharing a birthday with you or being excited about your photography. Now Lily is involved with something that excites her. Have you once told her how proud you are of her for getting a part in the school play? And not just any part, the part she wanted. Or how eager you are to see her in the play? Being a friend means caring enough to be willing to give more than you get."

Lucy felt ashamed of herself. When she thought about it she realized that she was the one always in need of what Lily could give her, not really giving back the things that Lily needed.

"I'm not even sure what Lily needs from me," she said out loud before she realized she had actually said it instead of it being a thought in her head.

"Maybe," he answered. "She just needs you to be her friend."

Sunday night Lucy called Lily and talked with her for an hour about *The Wizard of Oz*, Glinda and the cowardly lion.

Lucy arrived at the photography class early and took a seat in the second row. The first row was where the students who wanted to be teacher's pet sat, constantly raising their hands to be noticed. The last row was where the students who rarely paid attention sat, although Lucy didn't know why anyone would voluntarily take this class and then not pay attention. The third row was where she normally sat. It's the row you sat when you didn't want to be noticed. So the fact that she had moved herself up to the second row, the row that said you were interested but you weren't going to be insufferable about it, was a clear sign about how she felt about herself on the first day of this class.

People were filing in now, young and old, male and female, skin tones both light and dark, all carrying cameras and supplies and looking confident. For the first time since she had heard about this class, she was nervous. Lucy wished she had chosen the third row.

A stocky man came in, his arms full, and dropped the load he was carrying onto the desk at the front of the class. He removed his coat and gloves draping the coat over the back of the chair behind the desk. He glanced down at a piece of paper and then scanned his audience. He grabbed an armload of the books from the desk and dropped one on the table in front of each student calling out "good morning" as he went down the rows.

When he returned to the front he announced, "This is a beginning photography class. If you're here for a painting or cooking class, you're in the wrong place. Get the picture."

A weak chuckle ran through the class.

"Wow," the teacher said. "I obviously need to work on my jokes. So, if everyone is supposed to be here, let's get started. My name is Seth Nelson."

After class on her way out the door, Lucy ran into Michael Service.

"How was your first day of class Lucy?" he asked.

She couldn't believe that he remembered her name.

"Overwhelming, but good," she said shyly.

"I stopped by your grandfather's bookstore the other day and saw your photographs on the wall," he added. "You have a natural talent Lucy. I think you'll get a lot out of the class. See you next Saturday."

He walked off to talk with someone else before she could answer him. She opened the door and met the cold air head on. She didn't know why, but for once it didn't feel that cold.

When she arrived at the bookstore, her grandfather was with a customer but pointed up at the wall behind him. There was an empty spot where one of her photographs had hung.

Chapter 15

Lucy was having a hard time keeping up with school and the photography class. She felt exhausted, but was determined to make it all work. The performance of the middle school's version of *The Wizard of Oz* was only a week away and Lucy had only communicated with Lily by phone or by quick exchanges in the hallway at school. Lucy purchased tickets for herself and her grandfather for Saturday night's performance.

"Don't come Friday night," Lily had said. "It's our first performance in front of an audience and I'm sure we'll have a few bugs to work out. Saturday should be exquisite! Or you can come to the matinee on Sunday."

Another print had sold, so Lucy took some of the money from the two sold photographs and paid back her grandfather for the supplies he had purchased to print, frame and matte the first ten photos. At first he wouldn't take it, but she had insisted and finally he'd given in and taken the money. She still owed him a little more, but she had to buy some more supplies for the class. Lucy also wanted to print two new photos to replace the ones that were sold, but that would cost more money. She was beginning to think that she had taken on more than she could handle.

The night of the play, Lucy was having a hard time keeping her eyes open. She had stayed up late Friday night trying to get her school homework finished so she could concentrate on the work required from the photography class. The class that Saturday had been especially challenging for her and she had poured over that section of the book for hours after class. Now she just preferred to curl up and go to sleep, but it was Lily's big night and she couldn't miss it.

Her grandfather led her down the aisle to their seats and she read through the booklet they had been given at the door. She found Lily's name next to Glinda, the Good Witch of the North. Lucy had brought her camera so she could record the event for her friend.

The lights dimmed and the curtains parted and there was Dorothy holding Toto and singing, *Somewhere Over the Rainbow*. Lucy felt herself drift into a sleep but woke when her head dropped suddenly. She repositioned herself in the chair and watched Dorothy as she met up with the scarecrow, tin man and the not so courageous lion. Lucy was startled when the Wicked Witch cackled and she looked over at her grandfather who appeared to be enjoying the show. The last thing she remembered before falling asleep was the foursome singing *we're off to see the Wizard, the wonderful Wizard of Oz* until the sound of clapping woke her up.

Lucy looked around confused. Everyone was standing up and clapping. She had fallen asleep and hadn't taken even one photograph of Lily. She hadn't even seen Lily's part in the play. It was her time to give back to Lily and she had failed her. She wished she could melt away like the wicked witch. What was she going to say to Lily? Lily would never forgive her for this. It would be the end of their friendship.

"Grandpa, I don't feel well," Lucy lied.

"Don't you want to find Lily and congratulate her?" he asked bewildered. "She was wonderful."

That made Lucy feel even worse.

"No, Grandpa, I really don't feel well," she told him.

She was on her bed staring up at the ceiling. She hadn't said anything all the way home and her grandfather had been concerned about her, asking her questions about her illness. At home she had gone directly to her room not bothering to remove her clothes before collapsing on the bed. Her grandfather had knocked on the door to ask if she was sure she was OK. She had told him she just didn't feel well but was sure she'd be better in the morning and he hadn't said anything else. She was lying to her grandfather. She was sure that Lily expected her to call, but Lucy couldn't force herself to pick up the phone. And then what would she say? More lies.

Lucy started to cry. She had made a mess of her life. Lily and her grandfather had done so much for her and she had let them both down. She wanted to find someone to blame, her mother for running away from Alaska, her mother for dying, Carol for not letting her remain in Elm, her grandfather for bringing her here. Her crying had turned to sobs and she was using her pillow to drown the noise when she heard the knock at her door.

"Lucy," he said. "I want to come in."

She couldn't stop crying long enough to answer him. He opened the door and walked over to the side of the bed. It was dark, so he felt for an empty spot on the bed and then sat down. She pushed herself up on the bed and reached out to him. He held her tight and let her cry until finally she had cried herself out. Her eyes were puffy and she couldn't breathe through her nose.

"I ruined everything," she said through little gasps of breath.

"I'm sure whatever it is we can fix it together," he replied.

"Nobody can fix this."

She told him the whole story about being exhausted with school work, photography class projects and trying to assemble the photographs she was providing for sale at the bookstore. Then she lowered her head and told him about falling asleep during the play and never seeing Lily on stage.

"I wish you would have told me you were struggling with the work load," he said. "I knew you were studying late, but I thought you'd tell me if it got to be too much. You're thirteen years old. You have a lot a years to accomplish all the wonderful things I know you will do in your life. We need to sit down and work out a schedule that won't end up bringing you to tears like this. We can talk about it tomorrow. But now you need to get some sleep."

"What about Lily?" she said. "She'll never understand."

"Lucy, you give her no credit. Lily is a person who will always amaze you. In the morning, why don't I get you a ticket for the Sunday matinee performance. Sometimes people just need a second chance. Then, I suggest you tell Lily what happened. Be the type of friend you want her to be to you. I'm sure she'll be the friend you already know in your heart she is."

The next afternoon, Lucy sat in the auditorium and was Lily's biggest fan. She took so many photos of Lily, that the guy in back of her finally asked her to sit down. When the play ended, Lucy left the auditorium and waited for Lily at the door exiting the school. Finally Lucy saw her huddled around her family in the hallway and slowly walked up to her.

"You came on Sunday too!" Lily exclaimed. "What did you think? I thought maybe you'd call me last night."

"You were brilliant," Lucy said. "And I took tons of pictures. Can I talk to you or do you need to go with your family right now?"

"My parents are talking to the director," she answered. "We have a couple of minutes."

Lucy pulled her aside and nervously told her the story. She had a hard time looking at Lily afraid of the disappointment she would see there.

"I wish I could tell you how horrible I feel and how sorry I am," Lucy said. "You're my best friend and you've done everything for me. I feel like I failed you."

Lily smiled at her and then gave her a hug.

"You came today to see me," Lily said. "I'm sure you needed the time to do homework or work on your photography projects, but you came here instead. You took pictures of me that I know will be great. If you weren't my friend you wouldn't have told me the truth. We're not perfect, but we're best friends and I never forget that even when I get busy with things like this play. Plus, I know if I ever need forgiveness from you, you will give it to me without question."

Lucy hoped so.

Chapter 16

There were only three more Saturday sessions before the class ended and Lucy felt comfortable that she could handle the extra work until then. She agreed to only take photography classes in the summer, no longer trying to add them on top of her school obligations. Her grandfather told her that the eight remaining photographs hanging on his wall were enough for the time being and she could wait until summer to add to them. If she wanted to continue helping out some at the bookstore, that would have to wait until school was out as well. She happily agreed to all the concessions and soon found herself in a new, more relaxed routine.

She and Lily were able to spend a little more time together, although Lily had been spending a lot of time with Tommy. Lily's parents had strict rules about dating. Rule number one was that thirteen year old girls did not date. Tommy was allowed to visit Lily at her home fully chaperoned by her parents and her ana and ata.

"I've been practicing kissing so when Tommy finally has a chance to kiss me I won't kiss like a fish or something," Lily announced one afternoon in Lucy's bedroom.

"How do you practice kissing?" Lucy inquired feeling like a student in yet another one of Lily's classrooms.

"You can use a mirror, but then you have to clean it real good afterwards so no one knows what you were doing. So I prefer my arm. Here like this."

Lily gave her forearm a big kiss wiggling her lips around before coming to a conclusion with a loud smack.

"OK," Lily said. "Now you try it."

"I have no idea what you're doing."

"Here, put a little of this gloss on your lips. It will make them slippery and make the kissing part easier."

She handed Lucy a tube of lip gloss from her purse. Lucy put it on and handed it back.

"Go on," Lily said.

Lucy brought her arm up to her lips and quickly kissed it.

"No not like you're kissing your grandfather," Lily exclaimed.

"Yuck. Why would you say something like that!"

"Watch me."

Lily smeared her lips with the gloss and repeated the kissing demonstration for Lucy.

"OK," Lily said. "Now try it again."

This time when Lucy brought her lips to her arm, the gloss made an ice rink out of the event. She felt totally hopeless as her lips slid from one end of her arm to the other.

"Well," Lily said. "You need practice."

"Oh, my gosh, I forgot to tell you, Tommy has this friend who thinks you're cute." Lily said. "You know there's a dance at the end of the school and he wanted to know if you will hang out with him at the dance. Tommy and I will be there too, so it's not like you have to be there alone with him and try to make small talk and all."

"Who is it?" Lucy asked intrigued and a bit embarrassed that someone actually thought she was cute.

"Ted Whitehall," Lily answered. "He's in eighth grade too with Tommy."

"I'm not sure who he is," Lucy said.

"Well, he's kind of tall, has blondish hair, he plays trombone in the band I think. He seems really nice. And I think he's cute. Not as cute as Tommy, but cute as far as boys go."

"My grandpa will probably think I'm too young,"

"It's a school function. My parents are even chaperoning. It's a good excuse for them to spy on me. If you come with me and my parents, I'm sure he'll let you go. I can have my mom call if you think it'll help."

"I don't know," Lucy said. "What would I wear? My satin gown? My tiara? What about my diamond necklace?"

They were laughing now as Marty came to check on them.

"What's so funny?" he asked.

"Lucy has a boyfriend," Lily sang.

"No I don't Grandpa!" Lucy yelled. "Lily! She's just saying that because she wants me to go with her to this dance at the end of the school year."

She paused and then thought to add, "Her parents are chaperoning and taking her."

Marty tried hard to compose himself. His granddaughter had a boyfriend. First he had to deal with that episode on sex education and now a boyfriend. Kids were definitely growing up faster now then when he was young.

"I don't have a boyfriend Grandpa, really," Lucy said still trying to persuade him.

"Well," he said clearing his throat. "Tell me about this dance."

The school gym had been adorned with streamers and balloons. Lucy and Lily walked in with her parents and Lily waved at Tommy standing over by the refreshment table. Lily had introduced Ted and Lucy one day at school and now Lucy was watching him watching her.

Lily's mom had helped Lucy pick out a dress and her grandfather had paid for it. She told him she wanted to pay him back.

"What?" he had said grinning as she modeled the dress. "I can't buy my beautiful granddaughter a pretty dress?"

The boys left the refreshment table and headed in their direction.

"Mom, Dad, this is Ted Whitehall," Lily said.

Ted reached out his hand and shook Mr. Amaguk's hand. Then he reached for Lucy's hand and escorted her out to the dance floor.

Besides kissing lesson, Lily had tried to give Lucy dance lessons one afternoon. Lily had shaken her head at the site of Lucy trying to dance.

"Loosen up," she had said. "Like this."

She had demonstrated again moving her body in perfect tempo to the music. Then Lucy had tried again.

"Stop! Please stop!" Lily had yelled. "I think we need reinforcements."

Lily had left the room, returning with her mom.

"My mom is an excellent dancer," Lily had said proudly.

They had practiced the rest of the afternoon until Lily had declared Lucy presentable.

And here she was dancing with a boy who thought she was cute.

Marty drove over to the school. He hadn't planned on it and he knew that Lucy was in good hands with Ben and Rose Amaguk, but he suddenly had the urge to see her dancing in her new dress with a boy for the first time. He didn't know what to make of it when a teacher standing at the door to the gym wouldn't let him in. He wasn't signed up as a chaperone and he definitely wasn't one of the middle school students. He was glad for the safety and security the school provided, but he was devastated by not being allowed in. He heard a voice calling his name and Ben Amaguk came forward.

"Marty," he said extending his hand. "I'd ask you what you're doing here, but I'm pretty sure I know."

He turned to the teacher at the door.

"Phil, I can vouch for this guy, he's Lucy Wright's grandfather," Ben said.

Marty followed him into the gym and pointed to the dance floor where Lucy was dancing with Ted.

"They grow up fast, don't they," Ben said.

"I still think she's ten," Marty said in agreement.

Chapter 17

Summer finally arrived and each day the sun spent a little longer in the sky above Spruce. Lucy started her second photography class at the art studio with nothing else on her schedule to distract or exhaust her. Three more prints at the bookstore had sold and she had finished paying off her grandfather, putting the remaining funds away for her printer. But when she had signed up for the summer class, she was informed that a more advanced photo software program was required. She had used the money she had saved for the printer and had reluctantly asked her grandfather for the additional money. She felt like she would never come out ahead. The printer she had hoped to purchase remained a picture on her wall, a dream she couldn't quite make real.

On her way out of the studio after the first day of class, Lucy heard a voice behind her.

"Your name's Lucy isn't it?" the voice asked.

Lucy turned around and looked at the woman who had called her name.

"I'm Patricia Olsen, Patty," she continued. "I saw you at your mom's funeral."

"You knew my mom?" Lucy asked.

"We were best friends for a while. Well, for a long time actually. Do you want to grab a coke or something? There's a little place right around the corner."

Lucy wasn't sure what to do. She didn't know this woman, but she wanted to ask her about her mom. They were just going around the corner and they would be in a public place.

Patty was watching her.

"I'm sorry," Patty said. "I didn't mean to make you feel uncomfortable."

"No, I'm OK," Lucy said. "I just need to call my grandfather and let him know I'll be late."

She called her grandfather and told him she would be at class for about another 30 minutes. It wasn't exactly a lie. It just wasn't the exact truth.

She followed Patty around the corner to a quaint restaurant Lucy hadn't noticed before. The waitress came and Patty ordered a coffee. Lucy ordered a Coke. She thought she had just enough money in her purse to cover that and a small tip.

"I knew your mother was pregnant with you, but then she disappeared," Patty told her. "That was about . . . how old are you?"

"I'm thirteen," Lucy answered.

"That was about fourteen years ago."

"You said you were best friends with my mom?"

"Starting from when we were about your age. We were inseparable. Even when boys came on the scene, nothing got in the way of Wright-Olsen team. Your mom was the vibrant, outgoing one. I was quiet and reserved. What she ever saw in me, I never really knew."

The waitress brought their drinks and Patty added milk and sugar to her coffee, taking a sip and then setting it back down.

"That all changed our freshman year in college. We both had boyfriends. She was dating a guy by the name of Sam Kearney. They had started dating in high school, senior year. She was crazy about him. At least she was in high school. He was a soccer player and won a scholarship to the University. That's where we all ended up, Marilyn, me, Sam and my boyfriend Keith. I moved on campus, but she ended up staying at home. Well, most of the time. The first month of school, she would sometimes stay with me and my roommate so she could spend time with Sam. Then something changed. I thought she had met someone else, but she wouldn't talk about it. She stopped staying in the dorm with me and she stopped seeing Sam. Once I called her house looking for her and her parents thought she was staying with me. I ended up trying to convince them that I had just forgotten and I was expecting her at any time. I tried to meet her after her classes, but she would always have some excuse. She had an appointment, she had to go home, she was meeting Sam. I knew that last one was a lie. Sam had already come to me trying to find out why Marilyn wouldn't return his calls or see him. Finally I stopped trying. Then about two months later I saw her walking on campus and I ran up to see her. She was crying. I asked her what was wrong. At first she wouldn't answer me, but then I yelled at her to tell me what was wrong. She looked me in the eye and told me she was pregnant. I started asking her all of these questions, who was the father, what was she going to do, and then I told her I wanted to help. Then she just ran and I was left standing there wondering how we had gone from being best friends for all those years to this moment. Then she disappeared."

Patty stopped and took a drink of her coffee, but Lucy sensed she wasn't finished.

"A week or so later, your grandmother came to see me asking if I'd seen her. But I hadn't. She, your grandmother, told me that her clothes were gone from her room at home. I thought, maybe it was more like hoped, I'd get a letter from her, but I never did. And then fourteen years later, I saw *you* and Mr.

Wright standing at her gravesite. I'm sorry, Lucy, I probably shouldn't be saying these things to you. I miss her."

Patty took another sip of her coffee and was quiet.

"You don't look like your mother," she said studying Lucy.

"I wish you knew about my father," Lucy said.

"I don't, honestly Lucy," Patty replied. "I don't know why she never told anybody. What about your birth certificate?"

"My grandfather told me there's no name there, just *unknown*. I asked him. He told me what happened with my mom and him and my grandma. My mom told them that the man was married, that's why she wouldn't say anything."

"Oh!" Patty said, her word emerging as if someone had punched her in the stomach. "I didn't know that. But I don't understand why she left Spruce and Alaska."

"My grandma wanted to find out who my father was and my mom got really mad when she started asking around, so she left so grandma would stop trying."

"Oh."

For a moment silence hung between them.

"Why are you in the photography class?" Lucy asked when she ran out of things to say about her mother.

"Ah, good question," Patty said. "I graduated with an art degree and work in a gallery in Fairbanks. And I'm now just getting back into photography. I'm friends with Michael and John who own the studio. Their classes are the best, so I drive over here from Fairbanks on Saturdays."

Patty finished her coffee and set the cup down. Lucy had finished her coke some time ago, just biting on the straw for the last five minutes. The waitress came and offered them refills, but Lucy told her she had to get going. Lucy reached in her purse to pay.

"I've got it Lucy," Patty said handing the waitress money. "It's been nice talking with you. Well I guess I did most of the talking. Next time, I'd like to hear more about you. I'll see you next Saturday."

Lucy left the café and walked quickly toward the bookstore. Even after she had found out from her grandfather that he didn't know the name of her father, she had not lost the desire to find him. And if her mom's best friend didn't know either, Lucy was not sure where she would go next. She promised herself that she would talk to Lily about it sometime. She could never image not being friends with Lily, no matter what happened. Maybe Patty had felt the same way too. She shivered, pulled her hat down tighter and ran the last block.

Lucy was learning so many cool things to do with photographs in her class, but her favorite was working with color. She could add sunny skies to a cloudy day, she could change color to black and white leaving one item behind as a spotlight of color in the photograph, she could create a sepia tone giving a photo a special effect of being old. She experimented with photographs she had previously taken and with new ones she had taken as class assignments. Lucy had so many ideas for photographs she wanted to have matted and framed for the bookstore, but she still didn't have the money to do it. Her meager allowance gave her just enough to buy supplies for school and she still hadn't paid her grandfather back in full for the photography software. She thought about the printer she wanted to buy. She was pretty sure she would never see that printer.

The wall at the bookstore now held five remaining photographs. Lucy wanted to ask her grandfather for the money to add some of her new photographs for sale, but it had been her idea to pay for everything. So she felt caught in a tug of war with herself. She thought if the other photos sold, then she'd be able to pay him in full and possibly complete a couple more photographs using some of the new techniques she had learned. She willed herself to stop thinking about it, and let her mind go to other things.

Ted had called Lucy a couple times over the summer. He would be going to high school next year and she wasn't sure how all that would work out. Tommy was spending a lot of time at Lily's over the summer. Lily had told her that they had finally kissed and it had been pretty much what she expected. But Lily would face the same situation. Tommy would be gone from middle school as well. Eighth grade was already becoming complicated.

As summers often do in Alaska, this one took on wings and flew across the sun filled sky until it landed on the door of the new school year.

Lily was spending the last Sunday of the summer holiday with Lucy sitting at the edge of the stream behind the house.

"Look at us," Lily said. "We're going to be fourteen this year. We're starting the eighth grade, we have boyfriends and all is well in the land of the midnight sun."

She leaned back on her elbows and stared up at the sky.

"I got inside scoop that this year's play is going to be *Oliver Twist*," Lily said. "If that's the case, I'm going out for the part of Oliver."

"That's a boy part isn't it?" Lucy asked.

"Just because the character's name is Oliver doesn't mean it has to be played by a boy. In fact, now that I think about it, maybe I should get them to change the name of the play to Olivia. Now wouldn't that stir things up?"

"I want to see if I can find out who my father is," Lucy said changing the subject.

Lucy sat up with a snap.

"Now we're talking!" Lily exclaimed. "Things were just starting to get a little boring around here."

"You can't possibly be bored," Lucy replied. "Please don't say that."

"Why, why can't I say I'm bored."

"Just don't. I don't want to talk about it."

"OK, let's talk about your father."

"We already know his name's not on my birth certificate, and my grandfather doesn't know and my mom's best friend doesn't know. Who else do we ask?"

"If we had a picture of everyone who was at the University that year, we could see if you look like any of the guys."

Lily paused, but Lucy didn't know if she was doing it for effect or if she was thinking about what she had just said.

"Do they have yearbooks in college?" Lily continued looking excited. "We'll get the yearbook for that year and look at the pictures! This is a brilliant idea! Wait. Have you ever seen the movie *The Trouble With Angels*? It's really old, but I saw it once and the girl that was in it, I forget her name, well, anyway, whenever she had a brilliant idea, she would say, 'I have a scathingly brilliant idea.' That's what this is, a scathingly brilliant idea."

"Do you even know what scathingly means?" Lucy asked.

"Sure it means heavenly or divine or something like that. This girl in the movie was going to be a nun so it has to be something like that. What year was that?"

"What year was the movie?"

"No! What year was your mother at the University? I have to know what book we need."

"Well, I'm thirteen, so I guess fourteen years ago. How are we going to get it, the book?"

"There'll be a copy in the University library," Lily said.

"How are we going to get a book in the library at the University?"

"I'm working on that."

"I could ask Patty if she has one," Lucy said.

"Now you're talking!" Lily yelled. "Scathingly brilliant!"

Lucy dumped out the contents of her purse on her bed. She had dropped Patty's business card in her purse the afternoon they had met at the café and then had forgotten about it. Now she pulled it out and looked at it. Lucy picked up her phone and dialed the number.

When someone answered Lucy asked, "Is Patty Olsen there?"

"Sure, can I tell her whose calling?" the person replied.

"Lucy Wright."

"One moment please."

Lucy waited listening to sounds in the background she couldn't make out.

"Lucy!" Patty said. "How great to hear from you. Has school started? You're in the eighth grade now right?"

"Yes. School has started."

"Is there something I can do for you?"

"Well, I'm calling to see if you have a yearbook from the year my mom was at the University?"

"I'm sure I still have it somewhere, but I don't think your mom is in it. She left before pictures were taken."

"That's OK."

Lucy hadn't practiced this conversation because she hadn't been able to imagine what Patty would ask her. Now she felt uncomfortable. She just wanted to see the book, not have to answer a bunch of questions why she wanted it. There was a pause before Patty spoke again.

"You think it will help you find your father?"

"I just thought I would look through it."

"I don't see how it could help you, but I would be happy to get it to you. I start another class at the studio in two weeks, I can bring it buy the bookstore after class, unless you'll be in the class?"

"I'm not taking a photography class while I have regular school. I didn't think of how I would actually get it from you."

"I don't mind bringing it to your grandfather's bookstore. I haven't been in it for ages and I wouldn't mind checking it out again."

Lucy didn't know what to do or say. This wasn't going to work out. She didn't want her grandfather to know, at least not yet. If she left the store to meet Patty at the studio she'd have to find an excuse for that. Oh, why hadn't she thought this whole thing through?

"Lucy?" Patty asked. "Are you still there?"

"I'm here. I just didn't want my grandfather to know. Not just yet. I don't want to hurt his feelings. Especially since this probably won't help anyway."

"Tell you what. I'll come to the bookstore on Saturday after class. You know what time we get out. I'll just walk in and look around. You can walk by me and I'll hand you the book. I won't even have to say anything to you."

"Thank you Patty. How will I get it back to you?"

"There's no hurry. Just call me when you're finished and we'll figure it out."

They ended the call and Lucy sat there picturing how many ways this could go wrong.

Chapter 18

Lucy was in the back room at the bookstore, her school books stacked untouched on the desk. She was working on special effects on two pictures. She had started with the one of the moose, that first photo she had taken the day the moose crashed through the classroom window. She removed the color turning the photo to black and white except for the eyes of the moose, the eyes that haunted her still. She made them a deeper brown which magnified the gold flecks and they seemed to pop out of the photograph drawing attention to what Lucy saw there. She printed it on glossy photo paper in 8-1/2 X 11. Then studied it, made an adjustment and printed it again. She continued this process one more time until the photo looked the way she had pictured it in her head. The second photo was of her and Lily's feet in the freezing creek, little fish just arriving to investigate, right before they had pulled them out, the cold becoming too intense. On this photo she used a sepia tone effect, except for the toenails which she painted a shocking pink. She printed it, adjusted the color of the pink and reprinted the photo inspecting the results as if she were a forger verifying that this copy couldn't be distinguished from some priceless original.

Lucy was holding up the final copies of each photograph when her grandfather walked into the room. She had been concentrating so hard on her work that she hadn't heard him. He stood absolutely still, mesmerized by what she had done.

"We should frame those two to sell," he said. "They're, what's the word I'm looking for, they're hypnotic."

"Grandpa, I don't have any money," she said. "I still owe you."

"Let me explain to you about new businesses," he said laughing. "Just consider me your bank. I know a good investment when I see it.

"There are only four more photographs currently on the wall," he said. "One more sold today. Do you have any more like this?"

"These are the only two that are complete. But I had an idea for a picture I took of an ice sculpture when we were in Fairbanks."

She searched for it on the computer and brought up a photo of a Raven holding a fish in its beak.

"See the background behind it, all those trees?" she asked. "I want to make the whole background solid black and then color the fish leaving the Raven the icy color of mirrored glass. I'm seeing the fish as gold. I know it's not a gold fish, but I see the gold against the silver of the ice sculpture and the black of the background."

"Let's matte and frame those three," he said.

Lucy had to wait until Saturday to complete the work on the three photographs. When Joe came in, she and her grandfather left to have the photos printed, to purchase the frames and to have the mattes made. She signed and numbered the photos and added the information to the log she was keeping. Because she had sold so few of the photographs, she had yet to repeat any of the pictures. So all she had completed was 1 of 25. That was the number of prints they decided she would ultimately make of each photograph.

School had become a routine Lucy knew she had to accomplish but her heart was in her photography. She hadn't heard from Ted in a while, but in the back of her mind she had expected that. She did miss that part of him that made her feel like she belonged in the secret group, but any thoughts of that could easily be erased by her true love, photography. Lily told her that she and Tommy were still going strong, although she was seeing less of him since the school year had started.

When the school play for the year was announced, neither Lucy nor Lily was surprised to hear that a musical version of *Oliver Twist* had been chosen. Lily had practiced lines from the play all summer in anticipation of her audition, singing songs from the CD she had purchased, and generally driving her family to other areas of the house, except for her mom who would occasionally chime in on a chorus.

Lily had talked Lucy into sitting in the audience during the auditions, and Lucy was there now watching lines being read and songs being sung by a procession of classmates. Finally Lucy watched a boy walk on stage. He was dressed in worn clothing, pants just below his knee, a ragged shirt and jacket. His shoes were untied and a cap sat upon his head. The back of his hair hung below his cap and it appeared from where she was sitting that his face was smudged with dirt. The boy began to recite. His emotions rising as he pleaded with the audience. His accent was thick but understandable.

Lucy sat up straighter in her chair and stared at the boy. The teachers in the front row of the auditorium who were acting as the judges were all looking at one another and at the lists in front of them. They seemed confused.

"I'm sorry," one of them said. "My list says that Lily Amaguk was next to do a reading. Who are you?"

The boy looked into the auditorium and started to sing about looking for love, that same thick brogue flying off his tongue. No one interrupted him as his voice filled the room. Even as he finished the song, taking a bow, no one said a word.

Finally one of the judges stood up from his chair. "Would you please identify yourself," he said.

The boy walked to the front of the stage and took off his cap.

"It's Lily Amaguk," she said, bowing to the judges. "As Oliver Twist."

There were clapping and whistles coming from the observers in the audience and Lucy couldn't help but join in.

Chapter 19

Lucy was trying to look busy helping her grandfather put away a shipment of books that have arrived. She kept an eye on the front door of the bookshop and jumped every time the bell announced another customer. She was definitely not cut out for this spy stuff. Patty was due any time and Lucy was sure that this whole operation would fail miserably. Joe was at the front counter and her grandfather was in the back sorting through more of the shipment that had arrived that morning. Now would be a good time for Patty to show up, she thought.

Her cell phone rang and she quickly answered whispering into the phone. All she could hear was someone crying and a voice that sounded like Lily but the crying distorted the voice.

"He's breaking up with me," she said through sniffles. "He just called me and told me that he likes someone else."

"Lily, I'm so sorry," Lucy said watching the front door.

"I asked him who it was, but he just said I didn't know her. Then he told me she was a sophomore. He's in love with an older woman!"

Lucy had no idea how to console her, plus the timing of her call was particularly bad. Patty could walk into the shop at any time and she was tied up on the phone with Lily and didn't see an end to the conversation in the near future.

"Lucy, did you hear me?" Lily asked.

"Yes, oh, I'm sorry. I know how much you liked him."

"Liked him! I loved him! Now he's gone and broken my heart. I'm sure I'll never love again."

The bell on the front door rang and Patty walked in. Lucy looked up in panic.

"Lily can I call you right back?"

"What's more important than this?!"

"Please don't be mad. I'll call you right back."

Lucy closed her phone and looked at Patty who gazed up at her and then pretended to look around the store. Lucy heard Joe ask if he could be of assistance, but Patty said she just wanted to look around. Lucy pretended she was putting a book away and Patty came up to her gazing at the books on a shelf nearby. Then she quickly looked in both directions down the aisle, and seeing no one, passed the yearbook to Lucy. Lucy looked up and mouthed a thank you and Patty moved on down the aisle pulling a book out and opening its cover. Lucy placed the yearbook in an empty spot on the shelf in front of her and moved on in the opposite direction.

Just when Lucy felt confident that the undercover operation had gone off without a hitch, her grandfather emerged from the back room. He saw Patty immediately and stopped.

"Patty?" he asked not moving as he waited for an answer.

"Mr. Wright, how are you?" she said extending her hand as she walked toward him.

"I saw you at the gravesite. I'm sorry I didn't get a chance to talk with you. There were so many people."

"I understand. And I'm sorry, about Marilyn."

"Thank you. Do you live here? I haven't seen you."

"I live in Fairbanks. I work at an art gallery there. But I'm taking classes at the . . . at an art studio in Spruce."

She had almost slipped and said, "the art studio where Lucy attended classes," but caught herself.

"Webber-Ellis Art Studio," she continued.

"Lucy has taken classes there," he said surprised at the connection. "Lucy, are you over there? I want to introduce you to someone."

Lucy had been listening and wasn't sure if she should pretend she hadn't heard him or walk over there. An invisible hand pushed her and she walked to where her grandfather and Patty were standing.

"Oh, hi," Patty said acting surprised. "I think I was in class with you over the summer. I didn't realize you were Marilyn's daughter."

She smiled at Lucy and Lucy smiled back, the tightness in her shoulders melting into her back. Marty introduced them and they shook hands.

"I forgot how great this bookstore is. I used to come here all the time when I was at the University."

She stopped suddenly realizing what she was saying, but Marty either didn't notice or let it pass.

Marty said, "Well, I'm glad you dropped in. Feel free to look around, and if there's anything I can help you with, just let me know."

"Good to see you again Mr. Wright," Patty said. "And you too Lucy. It's nice to meet you."

"Marty," he said. "Call me Marty please."

Patty smiled and returned to looking around the bookstore. Marty stayed out in the store, so Lucy took the opportunity to grab the yearbook and take it to the back where she stuffed it in her book bag. She was giving up the spy game.

Patty picked up a book off of the shelf in front of her and read the inside of the cover. She turned it over, looked at the back of the book and carried it to the front counter where Marty now stood. Joe moved on to a customer who had entered the store and in the back room Lucy opened one of her school books she had brought with her. She started reading the first page of the assignment when something she read made her think of Lily. She quickly grabbed her phone and dialed Lily's number.

"What's so important that you had to hang up on me like that?" Lily asked.

Lucy could tell she was mad.

"I'm so, so, so sorry," Lucy said, "But Patty walked in with the yearbook and I panicked."

"Oh, my gosh!" Lily yelled. Then in a whisper asked, "You really have the yearbook?"

"Yes," Lucy whispered back. "I'm sorry about Tommy."

"That's OK. While I was waiting for you to call me back my mother gave me the you're-beautiful-and-will-have-tons-of-boyfriends-before-you-find-your-prince speech and I feel a little better. Plus someday when I'm a famous actress and he wants me back, I'll just tell him no, I'm in love with a younger man. Can you come over so we can start looking through the yearbook?"

"Joe's here so maybe I can get my grandfather to bring me over. I'll call you back."

Marty was ringing up the book for Patty.

"I'm giving you the friends and family discount," he told her.

"That's not necessary," she said. "But thank you."

While Patty was waiting for Marty to finish with the transaction, she looked up at the wall behind the counter.

She stopped on the photograph of the moose, then the one of the painted toes and finally the Raven in ice. She could see that they were signed, but couldn't read the signature.

"Whose photographs are those?" she asked, "They're quite incredible."

Marty turned around and stared with pride at the photographs.

"That's Lucy's work," he said.

"Really?" she said. "They're for sale?"

"Lucy's trying to raise money so she can continue with her photography courses. She insisted on paying for everything herself and I couldn't talk her out of it."

"I'd like to buy all three," she said.

Marty was stunned.

"I thought you were a photographer yourself and you said you worked in an art gallery," he said.

"I do, but there's something about these photographs. They're quite remarkable."

She paused and then added, "And no discount this time."

Chapter 20

They sat on Lily's bed and went through each page of the yearbook, putting little sticky notes next to any picture that had a resemblance to Lucy.

"You kind of look like him," Lily said.

Lucy replied, "I don't think I do."

"Well, we'll mark it and decide later."

They spent the afternoon going through the pictures of the students.

"We've marked thirty photos," Lucy said. "This is ridiculous."

"OK, you're right, thirty is a lot."

"We'll never find him this way."

"Let's look at the professors."

One by one they went through the photos of the professors. Lily would pick up the yearbook and hold each of the photos next to Lucy to see if there was a match.

"I'm not sure but you might look like this guy," Lily said finally. "But you're probably right, we need to find more people who knew your mom. What about her senior yearbook from high school? People write things in yearbooks like, 'see you this summer' and 'stay cool' or 'we had a blast in high school.' I've looked at my brother's yearbook. They really write stupid things. But maybe we could figure out who her closest friends were."

"I think there's still a box of her things in the garage. My grandpa moved some boxes out to the garage when we were fixing up my room. One of them said Marilyn on the outside of it."

"Now we're talking!" Lily exclaimed.

No one was surprised when Lily got the part of Oliver. Rehearsals had begun and Lucy and Lily had less time to spend together. Lucy hadn't figured out how to get out into the garage without her grandfather questioning what she was doing, so that project had come to a temporary stop. She hid Patty's yearbook under her mattress and would pull it out occasionally to look at the photographs she and Lily had marked. No matter how many times she stared at the photos, no note of familiarity arose.

She was surprised when her grandfather told her that Patty had purchased the new photos she had completed. In addition, one of the original photos had sold. He gave her the money and she paid him back what she still owed. He was paid in full, but now she had to work on more photographs for the bookstore so she would probably have to borrow from him again. But at least she wasn't as far in debt as she had been. She still had the picture of her printer on her bedroom wall. "Someday," she told the printer. "Someday."

It was nearing Christmas and Lucy had been helping her grandfather set up the displays for the holiday items which had been arriving in full force at the bookstore. She was reading some of the Alaska Christmas cards, laughing to herself, when the bell on the door rang and she looked up. He looked over at her and she quickly looked back down at the card in her hand. She remembered noticing him lately in her classes, but he must be a new student since she had not seen him prior to the recent sightings.

He walked up to her but she continued staring at the card in her hands watching him out of her peripheral vision. He picked up one of the cards on the table.

"I know you from school," he said. "I'm John Duran."

He waited for her to introduce herself. Finally she looked up from the card.

"Lucy."

"Nice to meet you Lucy. Are you shopping for Christmas cards?"

She put the card down quickly.

"My grandfather owns this bookstore. I was just looking at the cards."

She paused and looked at him and then remembered that he might be a customer looking for something.

"Is there something I can help you with?"

"Do you work here?" he asked.

"No, I just sometimes help out. If you're looking for something, I'll ask my grandfather to help you."

"No, not really. I just came in here to see you."

John Duran smiled at her and she couldn't stop staring into his eyes. They were chocolate brown with gold flecks like the eyes she had given the moose in the photograph. He was taller than she was which in itself was unusual as she stood at 5' 9" now. He had a chiseled face that reminded her of the nomads pictured in some history book she had seen in school. And she thought his smile could warm the coldest Alaska day.

Her grandfather appeared at the front of the store and walked toward them. He stopped suddenly looking up at the boy. He remembered that look. It was the one he remembered having the first time he had seen Anna.

Lucy looked up and saw her grandfather. She felt the blood rush to her cheeks and moved a step away from John.

"Grandpa," she said. "Uh, this is John."

"John Duran," John said extending his hand to Marty.

"Nice to meet you John," Marty said holding onto his hand a second longer than necessary as if trying to convey a message to the boy, this is my granddaughter and if you do anything to hurt her, I'll. . .

"John and I go to school together," Lucy told her grandfather.

"Are you new to Spruce, John?" Lucy asked remembering that she had only recently noticed him.

"My family just moved here from San Francisco," he said. "My father's a professor at the University. It's really cold here and dark. People in California think it's cold in San Francisco, but they should come here. I'm not sure I'll get used to it."

"You have to wear a lot of layers," Lucy said.

"I'll try that," John said looking at her again. "Well I have to get going. I'll see you in school Lucy."

He took his tall frame and walked out the door. Lucy was still watching him when her grandfather cleared his throat loudly. She quickly picked up cards from the table and rearranged them.

"What's next?" she asked as if the whole scene with John hadn't happened.

Marty wasn't sure and that's what scared him.

On the weekends, Lucy worked on creating four new photographs. She'd have to borrow a little more money from her grandfather to complete the framing, but she figured if she sold two more, she would finally be even with him. If the other photographs sold, she'd actually be ahead for the first time.

John had stopped to talk with Lucy in school a couple of times, once even carrying her books to class. He told her that he had tried the layered clothes suggestion and that he was a little warmer, but just a little.

"But how do you deal with the darkness?" he had asked her.

"I turn on all the lights in the house, which drives my grandfather crazy," she had answered him. "But wait until summer when you can go outside late at night and the sun will still be shining. The feeling is indescribable."

She told Lily about John, but then felt bad because Lucy wasn't sure Lily was totally over Tommy.

"Don't worry about me," Lily said. "I'm too busy with rehearsals to have the time for a boy anyway."

"Well, do you have time to come over and look at my mom's yearbook with me?" Lucy asked.

"Now, that I'll find time for," Lily said. "How about Sunday afternoon? I can have my dad drop me off. Did you get the yearbook out of the garage?"

"Not yet," Lucy said. "I haven't thought of a reason to be out there yet, so we need to come up with something by Sunday."

"He parks the Jeep in the garage, right?" Lily asked.

"Normally, yes."

"OK, I've got a scathingly brilliant idea."

"Grandpa, Lily and I are going out to the garage," Lucy said. "We're studying and I think I must have left the book in the Jeep."

Marty was sitting at the kitchen table working on orders for the bookstore. He looked up at them and smiled realizing he wasn't sure what she had said, but when Lucy and Lily walked on by, his memory caught up with him and he remembered she had said something about a book and the Jeep. It seemed to make sense, so he went back to studying the catalog in front of him.

The girls reached the garage and started laughing.

"Shhhh," Lucy said, "We need to find the box quickly."

The girls let their eyes roam over the contents of the garage.

"There's so much stuff here," Lily said. "I think I could spend days checking it all out."

"Well, we don't have all day," Lucy said. "So keep looking."

It only took Lucy a couple of minutes to spy the box.

"There it is," she said.

They unfolded the flaps and peered down into the box.

"Look at all this stuff," Lily said.

They were looking at books including a yearbook, a stuffed animal, photographs tied with a ribbon, a crushed and dried corsage, a graduation announcement, cards and a framed photo of two girls.

Lucy picked up the photo, "That's my mom and Patty."

"We need to look through all of this stuff," Lily said.

"We can't bring the box into the house," Lucy said. "Just grab the yearbook for now."

"But what about these photos?" Lily asked. "There could be a clue in one of the photographs."

"Fine!" Lucy said in a loud whisper.

Lucy grabbed the yearbook and the bundle of photographs and handed them to Lily. Then she reassembled the flaps on the box.

"Put those photographs under your sweater," Lucy said.

"But what about the yearbook?"

"I came out here to get a book. I need to bring one in."

The girls hurried into the house walking quickly and cautiously passed Marty.

"Got it," she said to him as they scurried down the hall to Lucy's bedroom.

"This stuff is a riot," Lily said as she read the remarks of Marilyn's high school friends.

Lucy tried to grab the book from her, but Lily pulled it away.

"*Stay as sweet as you are and good luck in the future*," Lily read. Oh, here's another one. *To a really good girl who's talkative. Good luck in your future years at college.*"

Lily looked at Lucy's face and saw pain there.

"Lucy, I'm so sorry," she said.

"I'm OK," Lucy said pausing. "I still miss her. But you're right, we have to read these if we're going to find out who my father is. Is there one from Patty?"

Lily thumbed through the pages at the front of the yearbook and then flipped it to the back.

"Here it is," Lily said. "*Well four long hard years are over. It seems like it was only yesterday that we were freshmen. I must say that high school really does a lot for a person. I didn't know many kids but it seemed like every year after that I meet more people. I hope all your dreams come true!*"

Lily looked up at Lucy, "That last part was underlined."

She found her place and continued, "*I know you have plenty of them. Remember all the fun times the four of us had. Good luck always! I know we'll have fun at school next year. Wish you were sharing a dorm room with me.*"

"She underlined *four*," Lily said. "*The four of us.* Who were the four of us?"

"Patty said they both had boyfriends. I don't remember Patty's boyfriend's name. My mom's was Sam something. I remembered that because he has the same name as our dog."

Lily was paging through the book looking for something written by a Sam.

"Here it is," Lily said. *"Marilyn, We've had some great times in H.S., but just think of the good times we'll have in college. Love Sam.* That doesn't sound very romantic to me."

Both girls were quiet for a moment. Lucy wondered if her mother was in love with this Sam. The way Patty talked, her mom had broken up with him early their freshman year at the University and Patty thought she was seeing someone else.

"Let's find his picture," Lily said.

They found the section with the senior's pictures. They studied Sam's photo.

"I don't think you look like him," Lily said. "But right down his last name. We might have to contact him."

This made Lucy stop. She hadn't thought about having to actually contact any of these people.

"I can't just call him up," she said.

"Let's just look him up on the Internet," Lily said. "Maybe we can send him an e-mail or something. Let's see if we can find out if he's even around here anymore. Here."

She handed Lucy a pad of paper.

"Write down his name Sam K-E-A-R-N-E-Y," she told Lucy. "Let's see if others wrote messages that would tell us whether they were a good friend. Then we can write down those names as well and look them up. The girls are going to be harder because their names may have changed if they got married."

They read through the longer notes and wrote down three names, Kim Chapman, Pam Jensen and Keith Burke.

"Hey, Keith sounds familiar," Lucy said. "I think Patty's boyfriend's name was Keith. I don't know if she said the last name. What did he write?"

Lily quoted, "*It's a pleasure to have you in our family. You take care of Sam cause you know how he is. Be good and remain as sweet and beautiful as you are. Good luck always sis. Hugs and kisses, Keith.* That's kind of strange calling her *our family* and *sis.*"

"Patty said they all hung out together," Lucy said. "Maybe they considered themselves like a family. Where are the photos?"

"Oh, I forgot," Lily said pulling them out of her waistband.

They spread the photos out on the bed.

"Look!" Lucy said excitedly. "That must be the four of them."

Lily flipped the photo over and read, "*Me, Sam, Patty and Keith, Prom.*"

They looked at each photo flipping it over for identification, but only about a half of them had names printed on the back. There were pictures of girls in what looked like a dorm room, two twin beds with posters on the wall. There was another picture of Sam standing in front of a sign identifying the University. There was a picture of Sam the dog in the back yard at the house and photos of people on what looked like the University campus. Most of those had no identifying names. One was of a man sitting on a bench with students walking in the background. He was looking up at the photographer and there was something in the way he looked at the camera that made Lucy feel like she had taken the picture, as if the picture was telling her something that no one else could see.

"What is it?" Lily asked.

"Nothing really," Lucy said. "Just a photo of a guy on a bench. Looks like at the University. There's no name on the back. It's hard to make out the guy's face."

Lily took the photograph from her and studied the picture.

"He looks older," she said. "Do you think he was a teacher? Where's Patty's yearbook?"

Lucy reached under her mattress, grabbed the book and handed it to Lily. Lily found the section with photos of the University staff and looked at each picture one by one.

"Whoever he is, he's not pictured here," Lily said. "Maybe he's just an older student."

"My mom told my grandparents that my dad was married with a family so he had to be older I guess," Lucy said feeling disheartened.

They heard the doorbell and the kitchen chair slide across the floor. Lily looked at her watch.

"That's my dad," she said.

The girls quickly gathered up the photos and the yearbooks and slid them under Lucy's mattress. They opened up their schools books, just as Marty knocked on the door. Marty opened the door to find the girls sitting on the bed studying.

"Lily, your dad's here," he said.

"I'm off," Lily said. "Lucy, give me that list we worked on."

Lucy looked at her confused for a minute.

"The list," Lily repeated.

"Oh, right," she said handing Lily the names they had written down. "The list."

Chapter 21

When the play was a week away, John asked Lucy to go with him to see the Saturday night performance. He had purchased two tickets in anticipation of her saying yes.

She wasn't sure what her grandpa would say. But she told John yes and decided to work out the details with her grandfather later. But later came sooner and she hadn't had the time to work on how she was going to bring it up to him.

"Are we going to the play on Saturday night?" he asked Lucy the next afternoon at the bookstore.

Lucy was dusting a bookshelf and pretended not to hear him with the hope of giving herself enough time to decide what to say.

"Lucy?" he asked.

She stopped and looked at him, then dropped her eyes to the floor.

"Grandpa, John, you remember John, you met him in the store, he asked me to go with him to the play on Saturday night," she said.

She started dusting again to give herself something to do besides look at his face. She was sure there would be disappointment there and she hated to disappoint her grandfather.

"How does this work, this dating thing with eighth graders?" he asked.

She stopped dusting and looked at him. "He said his dad would take us and then pick us up after the play. Well, actually, John wanted to take me for a Coke after the play. We can walk to the restaurant on the corner by school and then his dad would pick us up and bring me back home. Here."

She took a piece of paper out of her pocket and handed it to him.

"It's John's dad's name and phone number. John thought you might like to call him to verify all this."

"Well, that was very thoughtful of him," Marty said teasingly, taking the paper from her. "I'll call him this evening and then you and I can talk."

This was Lucy's first real date with no grownups present and Marty had been pacing the kitchen floor since he had hung up the phone with John's father. He felt comfortable that Lucy would be taken care of when it came to picking her up and bringing her home, but it was the stuff in the middle that ate at him. She was fourteen. He wondered how old Marilyn had been when she had first started to date, but he couldn't remember. He tried to remember his first date and the first time he had fallen in love at a young age, but that made him all the more crazy.

He went to her room and found her studying at the desk she had placed in front of the window. How she managed to get any studying done with that view, he had no idea, but it made her happy and she did get good grades in school so he didn't bother her about it.

"I just got off the phone with Pete Duran, John's father. He'll pick you up at 6:30 to take you and John to the play and then he'll have you back home no later than 10:00. That should give you enough time to have a something to drink after the play. Are you sure the restaurant is open that late?"

"John said he checked. Normally it's not, but with the play going on, it'll be open until 11:00."

She paused and then said, "Grandpa, don't worry."

He didn't tell her, but that was exactly what he would be doing.

Lucy looked beautiful. Those high cheek bones Marty had noticed when he'd first laid eyes on her had become a prominent feature on her face. She was only fourteen and she was already so tall. He wondered if she would continue to grow toward the sky. She had let her hair grow so it flowed down her back, that tiny flip at the ends still there. He noticed that she had been wearing mascara and lipstick, obvious influences from Lily. But she wore both sparingly, and it accentuated her beauty. Marty was pretty sure she still had no idea how stunning she was becoming. But he saw it and it made him worry all the more about John and every other boy who was sure to notice.

Both John and his father came to the door and Marty could see where John got his good looks. Marty insisted on taking a photo of them and then they were on their way, out of his control. His granddaughter was on the way to becoming a woman. It made him happy, but at the same time, tore at his heart.

Lucy and John found their seats in the auditorium and he reached for and found her hand. He laced his fingers in hers and let their hands rest on the arm between their chairs. When she looked over at him, he smiled at her and then leaned over and kissed her gently on the lips. Little butterflies danced in Lucy's stomach, kissing her ribs with their wings as they fluttered by. Then the lights dimmed in the auditorium and John gently squeezed her hand. "Lily," she told herself. "Think about Lily."

They were standing with the rest of the audience clapping so hard that her hands actually stung. Someone had walked on stage and handed Lily an armful of red roses. Lily smiled, waved to the crowd and then bowed, the roses clasped in her arms. John and Lucy exited the auditorium and Lucy told him that she would be back in a minute. She worked her way through the crowd to the back of the stage and found Lily surrounded by the rest of the cast.

"Lily!" she yelled and Lily turned around, running toward her and falling into her arms.

"You were brilliant!" Lucy said.

"Thanks. How's John?"

"He kissed me."

"Oh, Lucy, I'm so happy. Details later OK?"

"I'll try to remember," Lucy laughed.

She left Lily and returned to the front of the auditorium where John was waiting for her. She buttoned up her coat and wrapped her scarf around her neck.

"Ready?" he asked.

She smiled up at him and nodded. He grabbed her hand and they walked to the restaurant.

"OK, I'm freezing," he said quickening their pace.

"That was odd," Lucy whispered. "I feel perfectly warm."

The restaurant was crowded with theatre goers but they found a booth toward the back. She sat down in the booth and moved over to the middle, and then he slid in beside her.

"Will you share a piece of pie with me?" John said looking over the desserts listed on the menu. "What's Nagoonberry chiffon pie?"

"It's delicious. If you're going to live in Alaska, you have to try Nagoonberry pie."

"Do you want a Coke?"

He ordered for them and then picked up her hand and held it in his.

"Tell me about this Alaska of yours," he said.

She told him the story of how she had ended up living in Spruce, Alaska. He listened quietly as she explained how her mother had died and how she had discovered that she had a grandfather. She ate pie with him as she told him about her friend Lily and her love of photography. Then as she sipped her Coke, he told her about growing up in San Francisco. He loved to surf, hang out at the beach and bike on the trails around the city.

"When my dad announced that he had taken a job in Spruce, Alaska, I have to tell you, I wasn't a very happy kid. I have a little sister who's nine and she thought it would be adventurous. I just saw myself giving up all the things I love to do. So tell me what there is to do in Alaska."

Lucy told him about fishing and hiking, about ice sculptures and cross country skiing, about wildlife, national parks and the Denali trip she hoped to take with Lily and her grandparents.

"Well, that doesn't sound so bad," he said. "Look, there's my father. Is it really that time already? I've really enjoyed being with you Lucy. I hope we can do this again."

John brought her to the front door and they stood there, neither of them wanting the night to end.

"I'd kiss you again, but my dad's watching."

"That's OK, I'm sure my grandpa's watching too."

"Good night, Lucy Wright. I'll think about you until I see you again."

She walked into the house. Her grandfather was sitting in his chair pretending to read, but she could see that the book was upside down.

"How's the book?" she said.

He looked down at the book and quickly turned it over.

"Good. How was your night?"

She sat down on the couch and Sam came over and curled up at her feet.

"Lily was outstanding. I went back stage afterwards and congratulated her. John was nice. We had a good time. He told me about San Francisco and I told him about Alaska. I'm tired Grandpa. I'll tell you more tomorrow at breakfast."

She walked over to him and gave him a kiss on the cheek.

Sam looked up at her and then dropped his head back down between his paws.

"Night Sam," she said. "Goodnight Grandpa."

Marty began to breathe normally again. He had watched them from the window as they stood on the porch. He was glad that John hadn't tried to kiss her. At least he didn't have to worry about that yet.

Chapter 22

Lucy sat at the desk in her room looking out at the darkness. She was listening to John talk about surfing in California. She was concentrating on the rhythm of his voice, the rich tones of each word, the rise in volume as the story reached its high point. They talked every night, often for an hour or more. He came to the bookstore on the weekends and hung out with her as she tried to do homework or helped her grandfather with some chore. She had pushed her photography to the side even though her grandfather had suggested adding three more photographs at the bookstore. When she finished talking with John she would try studying but would grow tired and once or twice had fallen asleep at the desk. Lily called her, but it was always when Lucy was on the phone with John. Lucy would promise to call her back but too often she just forgot.

To Marty it was like watching a train wreck about to happen. John had become such an influence in her life, that Lucy had given away the other things that mattered to her without thought or consequence. Love, if this was love, was a powerful magnet, especially for a young girl like Lucy who still relied on others in determining her own worth. Marty knew he needed to tread carefully with her. The last thing he wanted was to drive a wedge between himself and Lucy.

"Lucy, what are the most important things to you?" Marty asked.

They had just finished washing the dishes after dinner and Lucy was getting ready to go to her room to wait for John's call.

"I'm not sure what you mean," she said.

"Well, how about photography or your friendship with Lily? Would they be on the list?"

"Sure."

"How about John? John seems important to you?"

"I like John."

"What else would be on your most important things list?"

"Well, you would be Grandpa."

"Could you give all your attention to photography and ignore Lily and John or me?"

"No, of course not."

"Could you spend all your time with Lily and stop taking photographs or spending time with John or me?"

"No."

"Could you hang out with me in the bookstore or at home all the time and forget about photography or Lily or John?"

"No, Grandpa, what are you trying to tell me? I really need to go study in my room."

"Could you give all your time to John even if it meant giving up Lily or your photography?"

She opened her mouth to say no, but her cell phone rang before she could get it out. She reached into her pocket and took it out, checking the screen for the caller's identity. John's name appeared on the screen. She looked up at her grandfather, but he had gone back to putting the dishes away. She answered the phone on her way to her bedroom.

John was talking to her, but this time she was thinking of other things besides the sound of his voice and the story he was telling. Lucy tried to remember the last time she had talked with Lily or had spent any time with her. She remembered that Lily had called her last week or the week before while she was talking to John, but she had called her back, hadn't she? And she was still taking pictures. Just last week she had taken one of a particularly beautiful sunset. It was still in her camera, but she would get to it soon. And her grandfather had offered to take her into Fairbanks to the restaurant of her choice last Sunday, but she had been waiting for a call from John and wanted to be alone when he called so she had told him maybe next week.

"Hey, are you there?" John asked.

"John, I'm sorry. I just have a lot of homework tonight."

"Can't you do it later?"

"It's already late."

"What's wrong Lucy?"

"Nothing. I just need to do something, I need to get my homework done."

"Well fine. I guess I'll see you tomorrow."

He hung up first. Usually they debated over who would hang up first. But this time he just hung up. She tried to study, but her grandfather's words kept coming back to her. She didn't want to think about it.

John was driving away from Spruce. She was sitting next to him.

"Why do we have to leave?" she asked.

"You'll understand when you're older," he said.

She turned and looked out the window and saw that they were now in Elm, Illinois, sitting in front of the house where she had lived with her mother.

"But how will Lily know where I am?" she asked.

"You have me," he told her.

They were walking up the stairs to the front door.

"I forgot my camera," she said wanting to cry.

"If you want a picture of the Northern Lights, I'll buy one for you," he said.

Now they were inside the house. She walked from room to room, but there was no furniture, just a pile of things in the middle of the living room floor. She walked up the stairs to her bedroom. When she opened the door, she saw the diary on top of her little desk. The pages were filled with writing. But as she flipped through it, the pages became blank. She heard the phone ring downstairs and she ran to the top of the stairs.

"Is that my grandpa?" she yelled down the stairs.

"Don't be silly, you don't have any grandparents," she heard him say.

The phone continued to ring. He hadn't picked up the phone and now the ringing was getting louder.

Suddenly, she woke up. She was in her bed in Spruce, Alaska, listening to the ringing of her alarm clock.

That morning Lucy put her camera in her book bag. As soon as she got to school she went to Lily's locker and found her there talking with a group of other kids. Lily looked up at her and walked over.

"Where's John?" Lily asked.

"I haven't talked with him yet today," Lucy said. "Lily, are you available this weekend to get together."

"Is John going to be gone?"

"Not that I know of."

Lily looked at her.

"What do you have in mind?" she asked.

"Well, my grandpa has been wanting to take me to a restaurant in Fairbanks. I would love it if you would come with us."

"I'll ask my parents, but I'm sure it'll be OK."

"Lily," she started to say just as the school bell rang.

Chapter 23

Lucy and Lily joined the others for the traditional walk down the aisle. They gave each other a hug and then headed in separate directions to wait for the graduation ceremony to commence. Their last names, Amaguk and Wright, kept them far apart when the seating was assigned alphabetically, but their separation would be short. Lucy was finally getting the Denali National Park trip that she and Lily had been talking about for four years and neither of them could keep their excitement contained.

John hadn't been thrilled that Lucy would be gone for a week at the beginning of summer, but then he hadn't been happy with Lucy spending less time with him in general. She tried to give him his share of her attention, but he never seemed happy with the limited access. She still cared for him, but there was something about his attachment to her that alarmed her. In addition to not seeing her, John wouldn't even be able to talk with her. Cell phone coverage within the Park was minimal at best, so Lucy was leaving her phone behind. The guides carried a satellite phone in case of emergencies and even Marty had succumbed to the knowledge that he wouldn't be able to talk with her as much as he would have liked. She had promised to call him, collect if necessary, when the itinerary took them to a destination with phones. At midweek they would be at the end of the Denali Road staying at the Denali Big Bear Lodge and

Lucy would be able to call her grandfather with reassurances that she was still alive.

Lucy was almost packed. She had purchased a waterproof bag for her camera and she and her grandfather had purchased gear and clothing she would need during the trip. She had to get everything in one large backpack and then be able to carry it all limited distances. Lily's grandparents, Clara and Pete, had sent them a checklist to help them pack correctly for the trip. Marty had talked with Pete and Clara for some time, mostly to reassure himself that his granddaughter would be in good hands. Even Rose had called him to confirm that her parents were really one of the top tour guides and adventure outfitters in all of Alaska with a perfect safety record. To Lucy it was just the best graduation present ever. She was looking forward to making a photographic journal of her adventure and to bringing back new photos that she could print for the bookstore wall.

At the end of the school year, Lucy had talked with Michael Service who had recommended she take a painting course over the summer. She thought the idea was a waste of her money and time. She was a photographer, not a painter. Then he had shown her works where artists had taken the mediums of photography and painting and melded them into an art form that had fascinated her. The class required a whole new array of materials, so she had been forced to go back to the First National Bank of Grandpa as she had begun calling him. She had only three days when she returned from the trip before the first day of class. John hadn't been thrilled about that either.

Lucy loaded her backpack into the Jeep. The sun had already been up for hours although Lucy yawned at the early hour of 5:00 a.m. Her grandfather had wanted to help her load her backpack into the Jeep, but Lucy had insisted that she get used to the idea of carrying it around. They drove to Lily's and were met by the whole Amaguk family, who were hugging and kissing Lily as she tried to escape the embrace of her kin. Marty was driving the two girls into Fairbanks to catch the train that would take them to their first stop, Nenana River Canyon, where they would meet the rest of the group scheduled for the seven day tour of Denali National Park. This was the only part of the trip where Lucy and Lily would not be chaperoned, but the train took them directly to their first day's destination where Pete and Clara would be waiting to pick them up. On the return trip, one week from today, Marty would be picking them up at the Visitor's Center at the entrance to the front country of Denali.

Lucy gave her grandfather a hug and she and Lily boarded the train. As they sat down Lucy reached over and pinched Lily on the arm. Lily squealed.

"It's real," Lucy said. "I just wanted to make sure it was real."

"Well, then you should have pinched yourself," Lily said rubbing the sore area on her arm.

Lucy watched other people find seats and get settled. Most seemed disorganized, carrying too many items onboard. She was glad she only had her backpack to contend with. She had taken her camera out before storing the backpack for the journey to Nenana and now pointed across the aisle and out the adjacent window, a blurry profile of Lily with the distance clearly defined and then a clear profile of Lily with the distance blurred. The train lurched and they were on the way to a part of Alaska she had yet to explore.

Trees filled her window and the land rose up around her. She studied each scene with a keen eye looking for the unobvious image. She would line up her camera to take the shot, but through the window she hadn't expected the photos to see what she was observing. She placed her camera in her lap and gazed with wonder at the scenery around her. If she could have taken away the sound of the train on the rails, Lucy would have felt like a bird in flight, soaring and winding through the tree lined valley. Lily's head was up against hers, both girls watching the passing miles, eyes wide with delight. After a while they sat back in their seats and talked about the trip that lay in front of them, listening to each other and to the steady rhythm of the train's wheels on the track.

Then they were crossing a bridge and the land broke free and fell to the bottom of a hole, a gorge so long that neither girl could see the end of it as each strained to see the entire view from the window of the train. Lucy brought her camera up to her eye and recorded the winding river cutting through the vast crevice in the earth.

The train began to slow and a voice announced the approach of their destination. They grabbed each other's hands, grinning so wide that it made them look like they had just gotten away with the most scathingly brilliant plan.

Pete and Clara saw them before the two girls had a chance to look, calling out Lily's name.

"Pete, Clara!" Lily yelled back running as fast as she could with her heavy backpack to give them each a hug.

Lucy followed behind her still getting used to the weight she was expected to carry although the brochure had said *limited*.

"Pete, Clara, I'd like you to meet my best friend, Lucy," Lily said.

Both Pete and Clara gave her a big hug. Pete picked up both of their backpacks with ease.

"This way to the bus, girls," Pete said.

"I'll stay and wait for the remaining guests," Clara said holding up a sign for Far Out Adventures.

"Lucy, you probably want to put your camera away safely in your backpack," Pete said. "You'll never be able to keep your camera dry during the rafting trip. We'll have staff along the way on shore who'll be taking photos so you'll have a record of the trip."

Both girls had dressed for the day's event of getting wet while bouncing down the river on an inflated boat. Lucy placed her camera carefully in its waterproof case and stowed it in her backpack. Pete took both backpacks and stowed them in the luggage area of the bus. Pete told them to board the bus and once everyone had arrived they'd be on their way.

The bus was small seating sixteen people and a driver. The girls walked on board and Pete introduced them to those who were already seated. He pointed to a young couple whose names were Rob and Laura, newlyweds from Spokane, Washington. Two men who were traveling together were introduced as Bob and Tom from New York. Pete introduced the remaining couple as Tom and Gail from Kansas City. Lucy thought they looked to be about her grandfather's age and she was concerned about them taking the rafting trip. But then Pete and Clara did this all the time and they were about the same age she thought. The bus driver's name was Sealy. He was a salty looking man, like the old man in the sea she had studied in English class, and Lucy thought the name fit him perfectly.

Finally Clara showed up leading the remaining travelers. Their bags were stowed and they boarded the bus looking around for empty seats. Clara introduced the newcomers. There was a family of four who had traveled from Florida, Joe and Tonya and their children Mike and Joe, Jr. And the final two travelers were sisters from Texas, Susan and Jean. Lucy loved the way the sisters said, 'Hi Y'all,' but she had already forgotten their names by the time they sat down. In fact, Lucy was sure she wouldn't remember any of the names, but found it interesting that she and Lily were the only ones in the group who actually lived in Alaska.

The bus began to pull away and Pete, who was sitting in the front of the bus with Clara, pulled out a microphone and began the story of what would become Lucy's incredible adventure into the beating heart of Alaska.

Chapter 24

The group, who had been divided into two and outfitted with safety equipment, was given the rules and procedures to follow once they boarded the rafts. Pete had explained that they would be oar rafting where the guide would control the raft from the center of the craft and they would basically just hold on for dear life. Lucy had already learned that Pete enjoyed being funny.

Lucy and Lily were in the first group that took off in calm water floating steadily with the current. As they seemed to glide over the icy water, Lucy wished she had her camera to take photographs of the passing vistas. But just as she felt herself fall into the quiet lull of the water beneath her, the boat began to speed up and bounce gently over small rapids appearing below them. She was packed in between Lucy and one of the sisters and the closeness of their bodies made her feel more secure. The bouncing became more pronounced as the river narrowed and fell toward its final destination somewhere many miles away. They were beginning to fly now, but not like a bird soaring smoothly through space. This was the type of flying she had experienced on the roller coaster at Six Flags in Illinois, but at least there you were locked in. The only safety harness she had now was the shoulders of Lily and the sister pressed tightly against hers.

The group was screaming and laughing as the guide expertly maneuvered them through the fast moving water. Lucy and Lily joined the group with vocal calls of fright and delight as the boat fought its way through the rapids. And just when they thought they couldn't take it anymore, the water leveled out, slowing to an easy glide. They took that moment to collect themselves and readjust their seating. The bouncing had moved everyone to a slightly different location in the raft from where they started. Lucy felt her muscles relax and took in a couple of breaths she was sure she had missed while the raft was flying down the river. She glanced up ahead and saw the river change a second before she felt the little boat pick up speed again. This time she started screaming in anticipation of what was coming. It startled Lily and she looked up ahead of them. Then she joined Lucy in the high picked squeal that could only be interpreted as girls having fun.

They continued down the river not sure at any given minute if they would be enjoying a nice relaxing cruise or a wild ride down an icy river. River water splashed up on their faces and Lucy was glad she had the waterproof jacket over her turtleneck and sweater. She wanted to see where the photographers were standing on the sides of the river taking pictures as the rafts headed downstream, but her eyes rarely were steady enough to view objects on the shoreline. The beautiful scenery in the valley flew by in spurts and it was hard to take it all in. But Lucy was having too much fun to complain about missed trees and cliffs.

Lucy was laughing so hard by the time the raft reached the end of the trip that it took her a minute to realize the boat had actually stopped. She looked over at Lily and saw she was also in a state of hysteria which made Lucy laugh all the harder. Finally they calmed down to a happy smile, and Lucy looked up to see that their bus had been moved to the pick-up location. Sealy was standing outside awaiting the group's return looking like a captain returning from the sea.

Each person took time exiting the boat, looking for stable ground to acclimate sea legs. Lucy's legs wobbled when she took her first step on land causing her to fall sideways. Pete's arms grabbed her just as she was about to go over saving her from the humiliation of having to be picked up from the ground.

She walked slowly to the bus feeling the coldness of the wind as it hit the parts of her that had gotten wet on the rafting trip. She entered the bus and the heat wrapped around her like an old friend. She took her seat as the second raft arrived and she watched the occupants stumble out and search for their land legs. She watched as one of the young boys tried to run to the bus too quickly after exiting the raft and found himself sitting on his butt on the rocky shore. She knew that would have been her if Pete hadn't been there to save her. By the time the last of the group found a seat on the bus, she was feeling warm and satisfied.

Pete got on the bus and asked, "Did everyone have a good time?"

Everyone cheered and Sealy put the bus in drive and slowly began to put the Nenana River in the rear view mirror.

They entered the Park making the first stop at the Visitor Center. The itinerary Lucy held in her hand indicated that they would tour the Center, watch a film about the Park, take a short bus ride to the Alaskan Huskies' kennels and then head to a camp for the night. If ever Lucy could have imaged a perfect day, this would definitely be it.

Lily and Lucy walked through the center discovering what they could expect to see as they toured the Park in the following days. Lucy was surprised at the number of different animals she could encounter on the trip. She knew about Bears and Caribou, but was surprised to learn she might also see Dall Sheep, Lynx,

Harriers and Ptarmigan, Alaska's state bird. She learned that the bears loved to eat blueberries that grew wild in the Park. The film talked about the environment of the Park and about safety while staying within its boundaries.

Then they were off on a Park bus for a brief ride to the kennels. At the kennels Lucy couldn't get enough of the dogs who loved the attention of the group. She cuddled as many as she could and snapped photos of each. They listened to a kennel manager who described these dogs as perfect for their jobs. "They love the cold and they love to run and pull," he said. He described the life and training of the sled dog and the importance of their job. It made Lucy miss Sam. After a couple more petting sessions with the dogs, the group was boarded back on the Park bus for the short return trip.

Their tour bus was waiting for them and the group entered the bus for the last ride of the day. Many in the party were beginning to show signs of weariness. Even Lucy could feel the events of the day and the early morning rise seep into her bones and she was feeling hungry all of a sudden. They had snacked on the train trip to Nenana River, but that had worn off some time ago.

The bus passed under a sign announcing their arrival at Healy Campground. It circled through the grounds coming to a stop in front of a group of nine tents, one for each pair plus a private tent for Sealy. On the way to the site, Pete had pointed out the public washrooms and had given them a safety speech about traveling to and from their campground in groups. He told them to yell *hey bear* as they navigated away from the safety of the group to use the restrooms, and Lucy wasn't sure if he was kidding or if this was an actual safety measure they needed to take.

Lucy and Lily ran to their tent and found it set up with a cot and a sleeping bag for each. There was a small table between the cots and a battery operated lantern. They plopped down on the cots, but then quickly got up to see what was happening outside. Sealy had unlocked the luggage compartment and he and Pete were delivering backpacks to the tents. The staff of Far Out had set up the tables for dinner and wonderful smells were filling the air around the campsite. Clara joined her staff giving directions while helping to set up for dinner.

"Why are you setting up the food so far from our tents?" Lucy asked.

"To keep the smell of food that might attract bears away from the tents," Clara said.

"When Pete told us to yell *hey bear* I thought maybe he was kidding us," Lucy said not sure if the tale was true.

Lucy ate heartily until she could no longer put another bite into her mouth. She couldn't move and sleep was beginning to weigh heavily on her eye lids. She and Lily were sitting around the campfire listening to the chatter of the group and the stories told by Pete, but even Lily's eyes had grown weary. Two of the couples had already turned in for the night, and as hard as they tried to extend the day by staying up, Lily and Lucy were fading fast. They finally gave up and headed to their tent. They each grabbed a towel, soap and toothbrush and headed with their lantern toward the washhouse. Off in the trees, they heard a limb snap and both girls stopped and looked around cautiously. They saw nothing and heard nothing further in the trees bordering the path. After a few minutes they began walking again toward their destination, this time yelling their advance, "Hey bear, hey bear."

Chapter 25

The next morning after a breakfast of salmon and eggs, the group packed up their belongings and found seats back on the bus. Sealy exited the Park driving past the Visitor Center they had explored the day before. A short drive later, the bus pulled into a camp where four Jeeps fitted with rugged looking tires awaited them.

"Is everyone ready for a little rock and roll?" Pete asked the group who cheered at the prospect of once again being thrown about on some wild and crazy ride.

The group was divided equally between the four Jeeps and Lucy and Lily joined the two young boys, Mike and Joe Jr. in one driven by a burly guy who introduced himself as Shep. Shep informed them that their trip would take them down the Gold Diggers Trail, a road carved through the trees by the early gold miners. When everyone was seated and strapped in, the Jeeps exited the camp and traveled along a blacktop road for a few miles before turning off onto an unpaved road. Shep told them that this was the beginning of Gold Diggers Trail. They bounced along the trail between the rolling tundra, swaying back and forth as the large tires bit into the earth. Lucy and Lily were laughing and Mike and Joe Jr. were hooting and hollering behind them.

After a while Lucy began to feel like her head would fall off her shoulders as the dips and turns became more pronounced.

She felt like one of those bobbing head dolls she had once seen on the dashboard of someone's car in Spruce. She had brought her camera, but there was no way she could hold it steady enough to take a picture, so she just held onto it tightly as it sat in her lap. The further down the trail the Jeep went the more primitive the road became. The Jeeps stopped occasionally, and in their Jeep, Shep told them about the history of the trail and gold mining. He pointed out interesting sites along the way, stopping once to point out a moose among the trees. Lily and Lucy looked from the moose to one another both remembering their previous encounter with this burly species. The Jeeps bounced along the rutted path weaving in and out of trees until they reached what appeared to be the end of the trail.

Lunch was being prepared by the staff of Far Out. Lucy had no idea how they had gotten the supplies to this location ahead of them. While the staff organized lunch, the group was taken on a short walking tour to a spot that looked across the Alaska Range. It was breathtaking, and Lucy finally got the opportunity to take a few photos. Far off into the distance she could see rain falling, but as she watched, it moved off to the east. As it did, the sun filtered through the remaining droplets of water left behind sending a rainbow of vibrant colors racing from the sky to the ground below. It looked so real, Lucy was sure there was a pot of gold just waiting for the first gold hunter lucky enough to stumble upon it. She brought her camera up to her eye and clicked the shutter.

During lunch, the guides told stories of gold mining pioneers and their families. Lucy could understand how so many of them died in the harsh Alaska winters. It made her sad to think about how many lives were lost to the promise of a better one. When the group was full of food and stories, they returned to the Jeeps, buckled themselves in and readied their bodies for the bumpy ride back down the rugged trail. Half way back, Joe Jr. leaned out of the Jeep and lost his lunch along the route. Shep pulled over to attend to him, but was surprised to see that Joe Jr. was all smiles and ready to go again. It made Lucy and Lily a little nervous as they were sitting in front of him, but he assured them that he now felt perfectly fine.

Back at the camp where they had boarded the Jeeps, Sealy was waiting for them in the bus so they staggered in and collapsed into their seats. Once everyone was on board, Sealy drove them back to the camp inside the Park for a second night out among the brilliant stars looking down on Alaska.

In the morning after breakfast they boarded the bus for the trip that would take them to the end of the Denali Park Road at Kantishna.

"I know you can all read your itinerary," Pete said. "But I want to take this time to go over today's trip into the part of Denali National Park known as the back country. Beginning at Savage River the road becomes restricted so you'll see less traffic and hopefully more wildlife. We'll be getting out at Sanctuary River, Teklanika River, Igloo Creek, Sable Pass and arrive at Polychrome in time for lunch, so get your cameras ready.

"*Bear* in mind, and don't be *sheep*ish, there could be *caribou* around every corner," Pete said with a straight face.

There was laughter throughout the bus and Sealy took this as his cue to put the bus in motion.

They had only gone a few miles when rain began to fall sending water dribbling down the windows of the bus. It was a slow steady rain, but the clouds became an obstacle for viewing the distant Range. Just before they reached Savage River the road dropped down and the clouds seemed to thicken around them. At Savage River the thick gray clouds made catching a glimpse of Mt. McKinley impossible. But the first treat of the day emerged when someone in the back of the bus yelled, "Bear!"

It had been one of the guys from New York and everyone turned to see where he was pointing. Sure enough, off into the not too distant landscape a grizzly bear was moving around in the brush. Lucy tried to zoom in with her camera but the bear only looked like a dark fuzzy blob over the top of the shrubs. Suddenly, it rose and looked around. She clicked the shutter on her camera as the bear stood staring in the direction of the bus. Now he towered over the bushes and dominated the scene, and just as quickly, apparently finding nothing of interest, the bear fell back down on all fours and began heading away from them. No one wanted to get out into the rain, so Sealy put the bus in gear and the group continued on their journey hoping for the clouds to break before they reached Teklanika River at mile marker 29.

On the drive Pete told stories of the Alaska gold rush, of adventurers and explorers and of tragedies in this harsh area of the world. The rain continued to come down, so they only stopped for a short stay at Teklanika River and Igloo Creek. By the time they reached Sable Pass, the rain had finally stopped. Everyone was glad to be able to stretch and got out of the bus. At Sable Pass Lucy stood gazing as far as the cloudy day would allow. She looked across the tundra to where the jagged mountains were covered in snow. She could just make it out through the clouds. She was breathing in the air when a hole appeared in the clouds and a beam of sunlight reached down to earth. It was as if the movie director had asked for a spotlight on the star because right at that spot where the sun hit the ground, a herd of caribou was grazing peacefully. Lucy called to the others and everyone followed the line of her arm to the spot where she was pointing. She heard cameras click but knew the group was too far away to be able to distinguish the presence of caribou on a 4 X 6 photograph.

Back in the bus, they headed for Polychrome, the stop for lunch. To Lucy the land between Sable Pass and Polychrome looked desolate. Clouds hung just above the ground as if there was some invisible force stopping them from falling to the ground. She thought it would make great black and white prints and had taken a couple shots at Sable Pass with that in mind.

At Polychrome they ran into a couple of hikers who were off for a two day hike. They had been hiking different areas along the Denali Park Road and reported seeing a Lynx and Dall Sheep. Pete informed the group that after lunch they would be crossing the Toklat River heading to Eielson Visitor Center and their best chance for a great view of Mt. McKinley, if the weather cooperated.

Lucy was getting anxious. The rain put a damper on the day's events and she was beginning to feel as gray as the skies looked. She had no idea what exactly she was expecting to happen, but this was far from the rush of rafting down the Nenana River, the thrill of soaring on the Alaskan railroad or the wild ride down Gold Diggers Trail. She knew she should feel privileged just being among the beauty of the Park, and maybe if the clouds would lift, her spirit would as well. Lily as usual seemed unaffected by the day, so Lucy kept this feeling she had to herself.

As they left Polychrome, Lucy stared out the window of the bus while Lily chattered on with Clara. The bus crossed the Toklat River and she thought even the river looked sad as it made its way over the rocky surface. She fell asleep as the bus wound its way down the road, through the vast expanse of Denali National Park.

She woke up when the bus stopped. She looked up and saw the sign for Eielson Visitor Center and it was like she awoke in another dimension. There were shadows on the ground. The clouds had departed to dampen someone else's day and the sun was filling the sky in its place. She joined the rest of her group exiting the bus and came to an abrupt stop as she looked out across the mountain range. Mt. McKinley rose into the sky as a frozen jagged rock, buried deep under bluish tinged snow. Her breath caught in her throat as she stared in wonder and admiration at its beauty. She realized her camera was in her hand and brought it up to her eye finding the right frame to capture the sun's reflection on the ice crystal coat draped over the mountain's peak. She moved the frame along the ragged cliffs searching for the unexpected. Soon she found a lone cloud wrapped around the neck of the peak as if it were a winter scarf placed there for warmth. In her view finder she watched as a purple hue appeared in the white snow. She snapped a picture and then it was gone leaving the snow without color.

Back in the bus Lucy's excitement had returned and she watched out the window in admiration as the scenery developed and then departed as they journeyed toward the end of civilization. The sights kept her deep in thought until she noticed the bus begin to slow.

The group had reached Kantishna and Lucy was surprised to see buildings constructed out of logs spring up from the surrounding nature. The largest building they were told was the Denali Big Bear Lodge containing two restaurants, a library and a gift shop. The smaller buildings were the cabins where they would be staying the next two nights.

The group was dropped off at the front entrance to the lodge. Clara escorted the group inside the brightly lighted interior where each couple was given a cabin number. After check-in they were shown to their cabins and told to meet back at the lodge at 5:30 for dinner. While Lucy and Lily checked out their room and adjoining bathroom, their backpacks arrived delivered by a staff member of Far Out along with photos from the rafting trip. Lucy lined the pillows against the headboard and sat back against them. She looked at the pictures, laughing aloud, and then handed them to Lily. While Lily was looking at the photos, Lucy picked up the trip itinerary.

"Tomorrow I think we have a choice of things to do," she said. "There's a hiking trip or fly fishing. Based on my experience fly fishing with my grandpa I think I'll pass on that. Or we can go panning for gold, but if the water is anything like the cold creek behind our house, I'll think I'll pass on that. But it might be fun to watch. What do you think?"

Before Lily could answer her there was a knock at their door. The two girls looked at each other and then Lily went over and opened the door.

"You should ask who it is first," said Clara. "Don't open the door unless you know who it is."

"Sorry, Clara," Lily said. "I guess I wasn't expecting a stranger out here at the end of the road."

"Well, girls," Clara said smiling. "Pete and I have a surprise for you tomorrow. Would you be interested in taking a flight-seeing trip?"

"Flight like in an airplane?" Lucy asked.

"Yes, flight like in an airplane," Clara answered. "We'll fly over Wonder Lake and you'll also get an exquisite view of Mt. McKinley. That is if the sun keeps shining."

"Oh, that would be marvelous," Lucy said.

Lucy looked over at Lily for consensus.

"Scathingly brilliant," Lily said.

"Lucy, don't forget you have to call your grandfather," Clara added. "There's a phone in the lodge you can use. Just ask at the front desk."

The phone at the bookstore rang and Marty picked it up. He was expecting Lucy to call him and he was anxious to hear from her. He hadn't been feeling well since the morning and had thought about calling Joe to fill in for him, but he had made arrangements with Lucy to call him at the bookstore.

"Northern Lights Books," he said into the phone.

"Marty?" the voice asked, then feeling confident she had the right person added, "This is Patty Olsen."

"Patty, it's nice to hear from you," Marty said. "Actually I was expecting Lucy. She and her friend, Lily Amaguk, went on a trip to Denali National Park with Lily's grandparents."

"I'm sure she's having a great time."

"Those two girls have been talking about that trip since the day they met four years ago, so I'm glad she's finally getting the chance to go. Are you looking for Lucy?"

"No, no, actually I wanted to talk with you. I'm sure you remember that I purchased those three photographs of Lucy's you had in your bookstore."

She paused and Marty said, "Yes, of course."

"Well, I hung them in the gallery I work at in Fairbanks. Not to sell. I indicated on the prints they weren't for sale. I was curious whether there would be any interest. Her work, for someone so young, is really special. Anyway, I had offers to purchase them. There was quite a bit of interest. Of course, I didn't sell them. But I could have. For three times what I paid."

There was another pause.

"I don't know what to say," Marty said.

"The reason I'm calling is that every year at the end of August we open the gallery to new talent. It's a one night event showcasing the works of Alaska's up and coming artists. We ask each artist to provide eight pieces and, of course, we work with them to determine the best pieces to show. I would help Lucy choose the pieces, and we would use a higher quality printing shop for her final products. Her photographs could be for sale and we would help her set the prices if she decides to offer them for purchase. We would work at a standard gallery commission if she chose this option. We can also cover all the initial costs if that's a problem for her. Obviously, if this is something you and she would be interested in, I will sit down with both of you and give you more specific details. Since our next show is almost three months away, she should have enough time to produce the eight photographs we would use for the show. Does this sound like something you and Lucy might want to pursue?"

"I'm not sure what to say other than I'm pleased for Lucy that you think so highly of her work. I'm sure I'll have questions, but let me have some time to think about it and discuss it with Lucy first."

"I'll give you my numbers. Marty, it's an honor to be asked to be a part of this exhibit. I know she's still young, but it could be the start of a great career for her. It could pay for special art classes, buy photography equipment and even help pay for college."

"Give me a little time for all this to soak in and I'll call you. But thank you for the offer, Patty."

"I look forward to hearing from you. And it was nice to talk with you again."

Marty hung up the phone. His arm was tingling from holding up the phone so he tried to shake it awake but the phone rang again.

"Northern Lights Books," he said.

"Grandpa, it's me!" Lucy yelled. "I'm having a fabulous time."

She proceeded to tell him about the rafting trip, the Jeep excursion, visiting the huskies and the trip along the Denali Park Road to Kantishna.

"And tomorrow Clara and Pete are taking me and Lily on a flight-seeing tour! If the weather holds out, I'll get a fantastic view of Mt. McKinley!"

"Lucy, I'm so glad you're having a great time."

"I am Grandpa. Thanks again for the trip. It's the best. Grandpa is everything OK with you? How's Sam?"

"Everything's fine. Sam's fine. I miss you and Sam misses you."

"I miss you too. Oh, Lily's telling me that dinner is ready so I gotta go Grandpa. I'll see you at the end of the week."

She hung up and he was still holding the phone in his hands when a customer walked through the door.

He helped the customer find a book, but he wasn't feeling much better and his arm was still bothering him. He thought he might have to close up the shop a little early which he hated to do. People expected you to be there during your business hours. But he just wasn't feeling well. He might have to make an exception.

The bell on the door rang announcing the arrival of another customer. This would be the last one, he thought. Then he would close up the shop early.

Marty walked out from behind the counter, looked up at the customer and collapsed on the floor of the bookstore.

Chapter 26

Lucy and Lily were beside themselves when they awoke the next morning. When Clara knocked on their door, the girls were dressed and ready to go.

"Girls, it's Clara, please open the door," said Clara.

Lucy didn't know why but the way she said those words reminded her of the night Carol came to her door with news about her mother. Lily raced to the door and flung it open.

Clara walked into the room and over to Lucy.

"Lucy, your grandfather is in the hospital," she said. "From what Rose told me, he going to be OK. He collapsed in the bookstore yesterday afternoon and was rushed to the hospital in Fairbanks. He's scheduled for surgery today. He had a heart attack, honey. But the doctors are confident that he will come through this just fine."

Lucy collapsed in a pile on the floor and started to cry.

Lily ran to her and held her.

"I've made arrangement for you to fly out of the Kantishna air field into Fairbanks," Clara said. "Rose will pick you up there and take you to the hospital."

"I want to go with her," Lily said.

"I already assumed that," Clara said. "Get your things together."

The view from the small plane as it made its way from Kantishna to Fairbanks was breathtaking, but Lucy saw none of it. She just continued to cry, holding Lily's hand until the plane touched down in Fairbanks. Rose met them and gave Lucy a big hug before hugging her own daughter.

"Let's get in the car," she said. "Then I'll give you an update. But he's doing well, Lucy."

In the car on the way to the hospital, Rose gave Lucy the details of what had happened and answered all of Lucy's questions.

"When he collapsed in the bookstore, a customer was there and called for emergency services immediately then attended to your grandfather," Rose said. "We are all just thankful that someone had been in the shop with him."

Lucy felt her heart skip a beat. She should have been in the shop with her grandfather, not off on this trip. She shuddered to think what would have happened if no one had been in the store.

"He was taken to Fairbanks Community Hospital where they determined that he had suffered a mild heart attack. He underwent an angioplasty. That's where they open the blocked artery to his heart. He's in recovery and will be at the hospital for a couple days then he'll have about two weeks of rest at home before he can go back to work. I've already talked to Joe and he's able to take full responsibility for the bookstore. It's summer and he's not taking any classes. He also said he would take Sam, but I haven't been able to get a key to the house yet. If you give me your key, I'll go get Sam and take him to Joe at the bookstore."

Still in a trance, Lucy fumbled in her backpack, found the key and handed it to Mrs. Amaguk.

"Lucy, you'll stay with us until your grandfather is feeling strong enough, and we'll make sure he has care at the house," Rose said.

"I want to take care of him at the house," Lucy said. "I'm going to take care of him."

"OK, OK," Rose replied. "We'll work all that out, but let's first get you to the hospital to see him. Lily, do you want to come with me or stay with Lucy?"

"I'll stay with Lucy, Mom," she said grabbing Lucy's hand.

The nurse let her peer at your grandfather through the glass in the ICU. To Lucy he looked much older than when she had left for the trip. He didn't look like the strong grandfather that she had come to know. The nurse escorted her back to the waiting room and explained that her grandfather would be moved out of the ICU to a regular patient room later in the day. Then Lucy would be able to see her grandfather.

"There's a cafeteria downstairs if you girls are hungry," the nurse said. "Just follow the yellow line on the floor."

"I know you probably don't feel like eating," Lily said to Lucy. "But you should try."

Lily directed her along the yellow line into the elevator and down one floor to the cafeteria. She put a mixture of food on the tray and sat down at a table, trying to get Lucy to eat.

"Lily, I should have been there, at the bookstore," Lucy said.

"Lucy, nothing you may or may not have done would have changed the outcome of this," Lily said. "So stop thinking like that. He's going to be fine. Just be thankful for that."

"I am thankful," she said. "But it's like . . ."

"I know," Lily said cutting her off. "Like waking up from a dream to find that you weren't dreaming or sleeping."

Three days later Mr. & Mrs. Amaguk drove Marty home from the hospital. A nurse had been scheduled to come to the house twice a day, but Lucy would be seeing to his needs between visits. She had insisted.

"What about your class?" Lily had asked on the way to the house.

"I'll call Michael and tell him I won't be able to attend this summer," Lucy said.

"Lucy, I think your grandfather will feel really bad if you don't go to the class," Rose said. "It's only a morning class isn't it? I can take you and pick you up. I'll be happy to stay with him while you're at class. Just think about it. You have a couple of days before you have to make that decision."

Lucy was sure that she wouldn't go. She had already left him once and look what had happened. When they arrived at the house, Lucy was surprised to see that everything had been set up for him. A hospital bed had been placed in his bedroom along with a table that held a pitcher of water, a glass and some books. Mr. Amaguk helped Marty into the bed showing him how to raise and lower the top section of the bed. Mrs. Amaguk showed Lucy the food that had been placed in the refrigerator for them, each meal carefully labeled.

"This should get you through about five days," Rose said. "If you need anything else, just let me know. And I mean it about the class. Please talk to your grandfather about it. I'm sure he'll insist you go."

Lucy looked from the food to Mrs. Amaguk and gave her a hug.

"You have been so good to me, to us," Lucy said. "I don't know how I could have done this without you. Thank you."

"Lucy, it's my pleasure," Rose said. "Remember, the nurse is due at 4:00. I'll call tonight and see how things are going. Are you sure you don't want me to stay for a little while?"

"I'll be fine. You've left me with everything I need."

After they had gone, Lucy went to her grandfather's room. She walked up to the bed and grabbed his hand, holding it in hers.

"I'm sorry, I messed up your trip," he said. "You've waited forever for that adventure."

"You didn't mess up anything," she said. "Besides one way trips are much more fun. Please get some sleep."

"I suppose you're trying to get back at me for all the times I sent you to bed earlier than you wanted to go," he laughed.

"Hmm, I never thought of it like that," she said. "Now go to sleep and I don't want to hear a peep out of you."

She kissed him on the forehead and closed the door on her way out. She went to her room and pulled out the yearbooks and pictures hidden beneath her mattress.

"Dad, are you here?" she said spreading the photos out across her bedspread.

"Grandpa, you have to eat a little of this," Lucy said.

"I'm just not very hungry," he said. "But I'll try. Here, hand it to me."

She placed the tray on his lap and sat down on the chair next to the bed.

"Doesn't your class start tomorrow?" he asked. "Do you have all the supplies you need."

"I've been thinking about canceling it," she said. "I need to be here with you."

"Absolutely not. I will be hurt if you don't go to the class. It's only mornings. I'm sure we can find someone to take you."

"Mrs. Amaguk already volunteered, but I told her that I was going to call and cancel."

"Lucy, please don't cancel. Go to your class. I'll be fine. I promise."

"But what if something happens to you while I'm gone."

"Nothing's going to happen. I'm feeling better every day."

"Then why aren't you eating?"

"I'm just not used to all this healthy food I have to eat now. It was very nice of Rose to go to all the trouble to make the types of food the doctor prescribed. See, I'm eating."

He picked up the spoon and placed the steamed carrots into his mouth.

"Are you absolutely sure?" she asked.

"I'm sure. Now what's for dessert?"

"Jello with bananas."

"Not exactly chocolate silk pie," he said rolling his eyes at her. "Oh, I can't believe I forgot to tell you something," he said. "While you were gone Patty called."

Lucy froze not sure what he was going to say next.

"She has an offer for you," he continued. "Each year the gallery she works at has a night for new artists to show their work. She asked if you would be interested. It's held at the end of August. You would have to supply eight photographs, I think she said, which she would help you with. Why don't you call her and talk with her and then we can see where to go from there. Would you be interested?"

"I guess, I don't know what to say. She wants my photographs to show at her gallery?"

"Lucy, your work is very good."

"Eight's a lot of pictures in between school and taking . ."

She stopped and dropped her eyes to the floor.

"You don't need to take care of me. I'm already feeling stronger, and the nurse comes twice a day. You can work on your photographs from home and I'll try not to bug you."

"I'll call her," she said finally. "Now finish your meal and I'll bring you your chocolate cream pie disguised as jello."

Lucy called Mrs. Amaguk and took her up on the offer to drive her to art class. Marty insisted that Rose not stay with him while Lucy was in class and she finally gave in. But she brought meals for five more days and placed them in the refrigerator.

John called and asked why she hadn't called after her trip. She told him what had happened expecting him to be understanding.

"I can't see you right now, but we can talk on the phone if you'd like," Lucy had said.

"If you can't make time to see me, I don't see where this relationship is going," he had replied.

She hadn't known what to say, and he had finally just hung up. He was acting so differently than when she had first met him. She wasn't sure what to make of this change in his personality.

Lucy struggled through the first day of class. She knew photography but painting was a foreign language to her. After class Michael Service stopped her on the way out the door and reassured her.

"Stick with it Lucy," he said. "I promise it will get easier and it will be worth it."

Mrs. Amaguk dropped her off at the house. She dumped her supplies in her room and then went to check on her grandfather.

"The nurse was here this morning and said I'm progressing like a twenty year old," he said grinning. "How was class?"

"Hard," she said. "I'm still not sure why I'm torturing myself by taking this class. But I did like the photos that Michael showed me using photography and painting, plus he stopped me after class and tried to reassure me, so I guess I'll stick with it. I'll make you lunch and then I'll call Patty."

"Call her first," he said. "I'm not starving and then we can talk about it over a nice lunch of something good for me I'm sure."

This time she rolled her eyes at him.

"Lucy, hi," Patty said when she came to the phone. "I'm so sorry about your grandfather. I was in the bookstore yesterday and Joe told me. I was going to call you at home today. How's he doing?"

"He's doing well thank you," Lucy said. "He told me about your conversation with him, about the gallery show."

"Oh, good," she said, "Let me tell you what I told him and then answer any questions you have."

She described the gallery show and what would be expected of each artist, how commissions would be paid if pieces sold and gave Lucy biographies of some of the other artists who would be participating. Lucy listened, asking questions when she didn't understand.

"I'm not sure I can get eight photographs done," Lucy said. "Eight that you would want for the show. I'm taking a painting class at the studio this summer. Michael thought it might be something I would want to try doing with my photographs. But after the first day of class, I'm not so sure. And I'm helping my grandfather until he's well enough."

"Well, we could use the three that I purchased," Patty said. "We can reprint and reframe them and you can sign and date them as originals. I'll show them as sold. I'll even pay you the difference between what I paid for the numbered copies and what we'll be asking for the originals at the gallery."

"You don't have to do that."

"Lucy, it's my pleasure. Why don't you start working on some photographs and you can send them to me as you get them finished. We'll choose five of the best and then I'll work with you and the printer for a final product."

"OK, I'll start working on them. Thanks again, Patty."

She hung up the phone just as her cell phone began to ring.

"Lucy, it's me," Lily said. "I got a reply."

"A reply to what?"

"Oh, I guess I forgot to tell you. I found some information on Keith on the Internet along with his e-mail and I sent him a note on-line. He replied back! He lives in Anchorage, but he's going to be in Spruce over the 4th of July holiday visiting relatives and he said he would like to meet us, well, really you. He also knows where Kim Chapman is. She's married, now it's Springfield, Kim Springfield. She lives in Fairbanks. Lucy, are you there?"

"I'm here. Did he say anything about my mom."

"No, just that he would be here and would meet us if we wanted to. We want to, don't we?"

"I guess so. But how are we going to do this?"

"I'll think of something. Do you want to call Kim?"

"I don't know. I guess I kinda forgot about this when my grandpa got sick."

"You still want to find your dad don't you?"

"Of course," she said to Lily but she was no longer so sure.

Chapter 27

On the third day of class, Lucy became intrigued when the teacher began describing a method called watercolor drybrush. After she heard the teacher describe the effect of color as *brilliant* and *vivid*, Lucy listened intently as the teacher explained the pros and cons of this method of painting and then demonstrated the technique. If she tried this approach on one of her photographs she would have to find the correct paper or canvas to support both mediums. She wouldn't have time to develop this for the gallery pieces, but it was something she felt she would like to pursue in the future.

After class she walked up to the front of the class and examined the painting the teacher had worked on during their session. She studied the effects of the layers of paint but then looked up when she heard her name. John was standing in the doorway to the classroom. Lucy looked at her watch. She had ten minutes before Rose would arrive to pick her up.

"John, what are you doing here?" she asked.

"Well, I never get to see you, so I thought this may be the only way."

She walked up to him, looking at his face. He hadn't called since basically he had hung up on her that first day she was back at home with her grandfather.

"Can we go somewhere?" he asked.

"Lily's mom is picking me up in ten minutes," she said.

"I don't understand why I am the last priority on your list."

"My grandfather had a heart attack. I'm taking care of him."

"Well, what about this class? You seem to have enough time for that."

She didn't know what to say to him. He was walking toward her.

"I thought you liked me," he said.

"I do."

"Then come with me now."

"How did you get here?"

"I rode my bike, but we can walk somewhere."

He reached her and was standing in front of her. She looked at her watch again.

"I can't."

"Can't or won't," he said grabbing her arm.

She tried to break free but he was holding on too tight.

"John, let go, you're hurting me," she said.

"Well, at least I have some affect on you."

She felt panic run through her body. She didn't understand what happened to the John who had taken her to the play and out afterwards. He was still holding her arm when Michael Service walked in.

"Let go of her," he said to John.

John looked over at Michael and let go of Lucy's arm.

"Lucy, do you know this person?" Michael asked.

Lucy shook her head no and, then nodded yes. "I know him from school," she said.

"Well, I'm going to have to ask him to leave," Michael said. "And if I ever see or hear about him harming you in any way, I'll have to . . ."

He stopped. Lucy wondered what he would have to do.

"Please leave now," he said looking straight at John.

John began walking out, then started to turn around but must have decided against it and continued out the classroom door. She heard the front door open and close.

"Are you sure you're OK?" Michael asked her.

Lucy shook her head yes.

"Do yourself a favor and put that kid behind you," he said.

Lucy tried her best to smile up at him and then continued walking toward the front door. She opened it and saw that Mrs. Amaguk was waiting for her. Lucy opened the car door and slid into the seat. Then she began to cry and she couldn't stop.

Mrs. Amaguk held her tight and let her cry for a couple of minutes. Finally Lucy pulled away from her, eyes red and swollen. Mrs. Amaguk reached in her handbag for a tissue, pulled one out of a small packet and handed it to Lucy.

"Lucy, tell me what happened," she said waiting for Lucy to dab her eyes and blow her nose.

"John. John came into the studio after class. He was mad and grabbed my arm. He's been mad I'm not spending more time with him."

"Oh, my! Are you hurt?"

"No. Michael saw it and yelled at him."

"Well thank God for that."

"John left after Michael yelled at him."

"Lucy, look at me. John sounds very possessive of you and that is not a good thing. There are many men and boys who would never do that to a woman. But unfortunately there are some who do. Lucy, think with your brain, not your heart. You should never allow someone to hurt you. Not physically and not emotionally, not ever. I'll tell you a story that Lily doesn't know so it will be our secret OK?"

"OK," Lucy said a tear rolling down her cheek.

"When I was in high school, I dated a boy who became very possessive of me. One day in the hall he got really mad because I had been talking to another boy and he slapped me across the face. I was stunned. He always told me he cared about me, but then he did something like that. I had a hard time understanding why he would do that. It left a welt on my cheek and my father saw it. I never knew exactly what happened, but that boy never bothered me again. I was heartbroken and it took a while for me to separate what I thought I felt for him and what he had done to me.

"Lucy, you can never accept this type of hurt. You are a beautiful, talented and kind person who deserves someone who will treat you with kindness, show you trust and respect you, and you will find that, honey."

Lucy looked over at Rose and then down at her lap.

"Please don't tell my Grandpa," Lucy said. "I don't want to make him upset. I don't want to give him another heart attack."

She started to cry again, but quickly wiped the tears away with the tissue in her hand.

"Lucy, I think he should know. But I agree that right now probably isn't the best time. Promise me that you won't see John anymore and that when your grandfather is feeling better, you'll tell him."

Lucy didn't say anything. She wasn't sure how she would ever tell her grandfather or what she would say to John if he called her.

"Lucy, I want you to promise me."

Finally she said, "I promise."

Lucy had begun working on the photographs she would show to Patty. Patty wanted to see her final products no later than July 15 and Lucy was sitting at her desk now going through her photo archives. She pulled up a photo of Lily. It wasn't a part of her project for Patty, but she wanted to work on it as a gift for Mr. & Mrs. Amaguk. Another one of her photos in the bookstore had sold while Joe was tending to the business, so now only two remained. But Lucy wouldn't have time to fill the space back up with her work. She was busy choosing the photographs for the art exhibit.

She looked at the photo of Lily working diligently to change it from color to black and white. It was a close up of only her face. Her black hair reflected the light and her long bangs fell as they always did to partially cover her right eye. The picture was all Lily with that grin that said another scathingly brilliant idea had just entered her head. Lucy played with the lighting and tones and then saved the picture to a file she called Lily for Rose. Then she went back to scanning through her photos.

She had already chosen two. Both were taken on her trip to Denali National Park. One was of Mt. McKinley where the lighting had turned for a brief moment to shades of purple and a scarf of clouds hung around the mountain's neck. She pulled it up and deepened the purple so it stood out even more against the contrast of the white mountain top and gray sky and clouds. When it met her expectations, she saved it to her art gallery file. The second was a picture she had taken just outside Sable Pass where the clouds hung above the ground like a marionette hanging from strings. On this photo she did her black and white magic so the dark popped against the light. She needed three more and paged through her collection thinking back through her time in Alaska.

A number of her photos of the Aurora Borealis appeared on the screen and it gave her an idea. She took four of the photos and placed them on one canvas using her software. One showed the colors of orange and green, a second one displayed colors of pink and purple, a third, black, green and yellow and the last, red and scarlet. She saw it as a framed print much larger than the size that was planned for the gallery showing. She would have to ask Patty about it. She looked through a couple more pages of photos, but nothing drew her attention, so she went back and pulled up the Lily photo. She saved it to the art gallery file and let her mind drift.

Lucy hadn't heard from John and in a way she was relieved. At the same time, she was sad. She liked having a boyfriend. She liked feeling a part of that club. She thought she had liked John. But she knew in her heart that Mrs. Amaguk was right, this wasn't the type of boyfriend she wanted. It was just hard.

The painting class progressed throughout the summer and Lucy came to realize that for the most part she was not very good at painting. Using the techniques to enhance photographs still intrigued her, but she hadn't had the time to explore that further, but it did give her an idea. She took a photo of a stand of trees along the Chena River and using software techniques began turning it into what looked like a painting. Texture appeared in the photograph like that of an oil painting done with knives instead of a brush. She worked on sections of the photo for an hour before she got it to look the way she had imagined it. Now finished, she saved it and closed down her computer.

Marty finally felt strong enough to go back to the bookstore. Joe had called him daily with updates while he was out and would be staying on full time for a little while until Marty was sure he could make it through a full day. The first couple of days he was only at the bookstore half days. Joe had done a remarkable job of running the business and Marty thanked him by handing him a sizable bonus.

"Marty this isn't necessary," Joe said. "I was glad to get the extra hours."

"I don't know what I would have done if you hadn't been here," Marty continued. "Plus you took Sam for two weeks. Just take it please. You earned it."

"All right, if you insist," Joe said stuffing the envelope into his pocket.

"I insist," Marty said patting him on the back.

Lucy was at Lily's and they were going over their July 4th strategy. Actually, as usual, it was Lily's strategy as Lucy had no idea how to pull it off.

"It's really too bad we can't set up your profile on one of the social networking sites," Lily said. "Are you sure your grandfather won't let you?"

"No way," Lucy said. "He read an article about this young girl who ended up running away to meet some man she thought was her age. They met on one of those sites, and it was not a happy ending. I can't remember which one, but anyway, it freaked out my grandfather and I got one of his speeches about being safe and careful and how there's danger all around me. I think if he found out I did something like that, I wouldn't get to see you again until we got to college. Besides I still haven't told him about what happened with John and I know your mom will ask me about that before long. It would all be too much for him and with his heart attack, I just can't do it. Maybe when I'm eighteen, if we still haven't found my dad."

"OK, let's concentrate on setting up our meeting with Sam Kearney," Lily said. "He's going to be at the festival in the park so here's my idea."

Lily told Lucy her idea.

"You're kidding right," Lucy said. "That's your detailed plan?"

"It's best to keep these things simple," Lily said. "Less likelihood of it going wrong. Oh, and don't forget the pictures we can't identify. I want to see if he can give us names for any of the unidentified photos.

"I also tried to find Kim Springfield in the phone book but there are too many Springfields. Do you believe that? So we'll ask Sam if he knows which one she is."

"If Patty doesn't know who my father is, I find it hard to believe that a boy she broke up with to date my father would know," Lucy said.

"Maybe he was jealous and followed her and saw who she was with," Lily said. "Did you ever think of that?"

"Do you think if he knew he would have kept that information to himself?" Lucy asked.

"Sure," Lily said. "Boys don't spread gossip like girls do. They hold it inside so they can blurt it all out fifteen years later to tough interrogators like us."

"You will be a famous actress some day," Lucy said rolling her eyes at Lily.

Chapter 28

July 4th celebrations in Spruce always saddened Lucy. With almost total daylight, the celebration lacked the one aspect that Lucy loved the most, fireworks. She could never get used to the festivities without the colorful bursts of fire lighting up the night sky. But the town of Spruce tried to make up for that in other ways that made the event special for the local citizens. The day started off with a parade, followed by concerts in the park, foods containing high quantities of sugar and fat, carnival rides and a bonfire later in the evening to take the place of fireworks. Although made with good intentions, a bonfire was not fireworks in Lucy's eyes.

Lucy arrived with her grandfather and they met the Amaguks at the start of the parade. Lily kept an eye on her watch. She and Lucy were meeting Sam right after the parade near the Ferris wheel. Both girls stood impatiently watching the procession of floats, cars and bands pass them by. Finally, the Spruce fire truck appeared signaling the end of the parade.

"We have to go to the bathroom," Lily told the group. "We'll meet you in front of the band shell."

Before any adult from the group could respond, Lily grabbed Lucy by the hand and they were off running through the crowd.

"That felt suspicious even to me," Lucy said when they finally slowed down.

"Trust me," Lily said. "They won't think anything of it. I'm always like that."

They reached the Ferris wheel and looked around for Sam. Lily saw a man walking toward them and she thought it looked like Sam from the pictures they had seen. He had a young girl about ten with him.

"Are you Lucy and Lily?" he asked as he approached them.

"Yes, I'm Lily and this is Lucy, Lucy Wright," Lily said.

Sam studied Lucy and then remembered the young girl standing next to him.

"This is Samantha, my daughter," Sam said. "Lucy, I expected you to look like your mother. I'm sorry about your loss."

"Thank you," Lucy said. "Everyone says I don't look like her."

"Which is why we asked you to meet us," Lily cut in. "Lucy's trying to find out who her father is, so we've been asking some of her mom's friends to see if they can help."

"I truly wish I could help you," Sam said. "But Marilyn and I, well, it didn't work out. I guess she started seeing someone else. Did you ask her best friend Patty Olsen?"

"We did," Lucy answered quietly. "We just thought you might know. We're sorry to bother you."

"No bother," he said. "It's nice to meet you."

"Wait!" Lucy cut in. "Can you look at a couple of photos and tell us if you know who the people are?"

"Sure," he said.

Lucy took the photos from her purse and handed them to him.

"Wow, look how young we looked," he said more to himself then to the three girls who watched him flip through the photographs. "Some of these are the kids we hung around with in high school. That's the back of me in this one. These are some of the girls in Patty's dorm."

He reached the photo of the man on the bench and studied it.

"I don't know who this is," he said. "Maybe a professor. It looks like it was taken on campus. But not a teacher that I remember, although he does look a little familiar. I'm sorry, I wish I could be more helpful. Did you try getting a yearbook from that year to see if he matched any of the photos of the teaching staff? That's the only thing I can think of if you really think this guy is important to your search."

"We don't know if he's important," Lucy said saddened that Sam could offer no information. "It's just a photo my mom had. And we did look at a yearbook, but he didn't match any photos in the staff section."

"Do you have a number for Kim Springfield," Lily asked Sam. "Do you know which one she is?"

Lily handed him a page out of a phone book she had taken out of her pocket. Sam skimmed the list.

"Robert Springfield," he said pointing to the name on the list of Springfields. "But they weren't that close after high school, so I would be surprised if she knows anything that would help you. I think she went to some school outside of Alaska for a while before coming back to the University."

"Do you know anyone else that she was friends with that might be able to help us?" Lily asked.

"She had a lot of friends but she was only really close with Patty. Marilyn and Patty had been friends for a long time, so if Patty doesn't know, I can't imagine that anyone else would. When Marilyn wanted something kept private, you can be pretty sure that no one knew about it. I'm sorry I couldn't help you."

"Thank you for meeting us," Lucy said.

Lucy was sorry for herself that she wasn't any closer to finding out who her father was. But she had also felt sorry for Samantha standing there listening to this conversation and not being a part of it. She wondered if Samantha figured out that her father had dated her mother. They could have been sisters. But Lucy knew she wasn't. Her mom had broken up with Sam more than a year before she was born and she didn't look at all like Samantha. In fact, she was beginning to feel like she didn't look like anyone.

They said their goodbyes and Lucy and Lily raced to the band shelter. The first group was setting up to play and Lily spotted her family sitting on blankets about half way into the crowd.

"I didn't think this through as well as I thought," Lily said as she waved at her mom who had spotted them.

"What do you mean?" asked Lucy. "We talked with Sam and now we're back here, and no one knows."

"Well that's true," Lily said. "But now I really do have to go to the bathroom."

Chapter 29

Lucy only had five more days to get her photographs together for Patty. Lily had called Kim, but Kim had basically repeated what Sam had said. She had gone to college in California for the first two years before returning to the University and had not talked with Marilyn since high school. There was still the Pam and Keith on the list that she and Lily had made, but she no longer had any hope that one of these people could offer significant information and she let the search drop for the time being. Lily, of course, was hugely disappointed, so Lucy told her if she came up with any additional ideas, she would resume the search.

Meanwhile, Lucy was at her computer scrolling through more photos. Sam came into her room and placed his head on her lap.

"Give me some inspiration Sam," she said.

But he only looked up at her, raising his eyes to see her without moving his head from her lap. Then he moved his head as if viewing the photographs with her.

"If you see one you like just bark," she said.

She chose a photo of the Northern Lights and experimented with turning the colors to black and white. She was looking for a spiritual look, but the light wasn't right in the picture. She needed vertical shafts of light not horizontal. Lucy looked for other photos she had taken of the Aurora Borealis until she found one she thought would be right. Again she removed the color changing the photo to black and white then played with the lighting until the photo looked the way the image had appeared in her mind. In the foreground, tall pines bathed in winter snow and in the background shafts of white light dancing down from the heavens. She smiled and Sam barked.

"I couldn't agree with you more," she told him.

Then she had another idea and poured through her photos for a forest of trees. When she found one, she turned the trunks of the trees in the foreground blue along with the sky, but the blue wasn't right. She searched her color palette until she found that right one, Bold Flock Blue. The trees in the background she colored green with specks of yellow and gold. She sat back in her chair and studied the photograph. It was interesting, but it wasn't one of her favorites. But she added to her art gallery file deciding to let Patty make the final decision.

She should be practicing her lessons from painting class, but her heart wasn't in it. She was thinking ahead to the gallery showing and to the beginning of high school. She and Lily would be starting in a new school again and they would both be turning fifteen. So much had changed in her life. She looked through her bedroom window and could just make out the long forgotten tree house. Until she had seen it from the kitchen window, she hadn't realized that it was also in this view.

Sam raised his head from her lap and left her room. Then she heard her grandfather open the door to the kitchen. She heard him place something on the countertop and then his footsteps as he made his way to her room.

"Hi," he said.

She was getting ready to turn around in her chair when her eyes caught sight of the tree house again.

"Did you build that for her?" she asked him not turning around to look at his face.

"Did I build what for whom?" he said laughing at her question that seemed to have no relevance.

"The tree house, did you build that tree house for my mom?"

Marty walked behind Lucy, leaned over the desk and looked out the window.

"Yes, when she was about seven. Even in high school I caught her sitting up there. Whenever she had to think something out, she'd go sit in that tree house."

"I think I know why my mom chose to live in a town named Elm. If she came from a town named Spruce maybe she was looking for the connection to the name of a tree. She told me a story once but at the time I thought it was just something she had made up. She said she always felt at home in the tree house she had when she was young. Something about magical things that happened when she escaped within its walls."

Lucy looked over at Marty. He was still staring at the tree house and she couldn't tell if it made him sad or happy. Sometimes those two expressions looked similar.

At dinner that night, the subject of John finally came up, but it wasn't Lucy who had initiated the conversation.

"I haven't heard you talk about John lately," Marty said to her. "Is he gone for the summer?"

She stared at her food. She had tried to practice how she would tell him, but nothing had ever sounded right in her mind. She heard Rose in her head saying, *promise me when your grandfather is feeling better, you'll tell him.*

"Grandpa, I'm not seeing John anymore," she said.

She wanted to leave it at that, but she could tell he was waiting for more. She stuffed a fork full of carrots into her mouth and started chewing them slowly. But he waited until she swallowed. She loaded up her fork with carrots again.

"Lucy," he said, the word stopping her from putting the carrots into her mouth.

She told him the whole story and watched as his expression turned from disbelief, to fear and then to hatred, something she had never seen in him before.

"Rose agreed I could wait to tell you until you were feeling better," she said. "Everything's fine now and I was afraid it would upset you. I was right, wasn't I?"

"Of course I'm upset," he said trying to keep his voice level. "If someone hurts you, I'm going to be upset. It's a natural feeling when you love someone."

"I'm sorry, Grandpa."

"You have nothing to be sorry about Lucy."

"It seems like I'm always in situations when you say that to me."

"I'm sorry that there are people who put you in situations where I have to say that. Are you OK?"

"I'm fine Grandpa. Really I am."

He got up from his chair and gave her a big hug.

"Now finish your carrots," he said.

She raised the fork to her lips, but stopped.

"I love you too," she said.

Chapter 30

Lucy loaded the pictures she had completed onto a CD and Marty drove her to the art gallery in Fairbanks for their meeting. They were met by Patty who introduced them both to the gallery owner, Marcia White.

"We're very impressed with your work Lucy," Marcia said. "And it's my pleasure to show your work as a new Alaska artist. In fact, since this is the 50th anniversary of Alaska's statehood, we've invited past new artists to this year's event. This gallery has been in Fairbanks for twenty-one years, so we are expecting quite a few artists, many of them quite famous now.

"Well, it was nice to meet you both," she continued glancing at her watch. "I'll leave you in the capable hands of Patty."

She shook their hands and Patty took them to a back office where she loaded Lucy's CD and lowered a screen which hung from the ceiling. She pulled up the first photo. The purple mountains with the cloud scarf filled the screen.

"I don't know why you chose this color of purple, but it's spellbinding," she said.

Next she viewed the black and white of the suspended clouds. She shook her head yes, but didn't say anything going on to the one with the four Northern Lights photos.

"I wasn't sure about that," Lucy said. "I saw it as a really large photo, not the smaller ones we talked about."

Patty made a sound like she was thinking about it, but went on to the next photo. The one of Lily popped up on the screen.

"Oh, I didn't mean for that one to be included," Lucy said. "It's a project I was working on for Lily's mom. She's been really good to me and I wanted to give it to her and Lily's dad as a gift."

"That's an incredible picture of Lily," Marty said.

Patty looked at the photo and then at Lucy.

"I might like to use it," Patty said. "But if it's a gift, we'd have to mark it as sold. But that would mean half of the photos you're displaying will be sold."

"Would it help if we told you to sell the ones you bought if that is something you would consider? Marty asked. "You obviously can keep any profit you make."

"I didn't want to do that, but let me talk with Marcia about it when I present the collection to her," Patty said.

Patty brought her attention back to the screen and pulled up the next picture, the one of the blue trees.

"Fascinating color," she said.

Next the photo of the tree stand appeared as an oil painting.

Patty examined it and continued on to the last photograph.

The ghost-like appearance of the Northern Lights made Marty gasp.

"Well, Lucy, I wasn't wrong about your work," Patty said. "You have a gift."

Marty took Lucy out to lunch in Fairbanks to celebrate. It was one of her favorites full of local business people grabbing lunch in the middle of their days. Marty didn't understand why this scene captivated her. It was too busy for him. He preferred something more quiet and slow.

"You know that saying that you used to say to my mom and that she said to me?" Lucy asked. "The one about life being like a drawer?"

She continued not giving him time to reply.

"When I lived in Illinois I used to think my life was uninteresting and I blamed it on Elm and probably on my mom and on everyone but myself. You helped me see that if I wanted my life to be one that would fill the pages of a diary, I was the only one who could do that. That's why I decided to find a way to take those photography classes. You opened my eyes to the things around me by giving me a camera and showing me that I was already seeing things the way my photographs showed. I just didn't pay attention to it before."

The waiter came to the table and they gave him their drink order.

"I'm so unlike the way my mom was growing up," she said. "Patty said she was the quiet one and my mom was the outgoing one. Kind of the opposite of me and Lily."

"When did you talk to Patty about your mom?" Marty asked.

"I guess one day at the art studio," she said trying to brush it off. This is why she hated secrets. She was never good at keeping them and they always had a way of popping out when you least expected them. But the art studio story must have seemed plausible, because her grandfather shook his head like he understood. That was one of Lily's new words, *plausible*. "If you make the story plausible," she would say, "it will be believable."

"Your mother was outgoing, but she was also quiet and reserved like you are," he said. "I think she spent a lot of time thinking about things. I think you spend a lot of time thinking about things."

They were quiet for a few minutes as they read the menus.

"Remember the first meal we had together?" she said.

"Sometimes like it was yesterday," he said with a big smile. "So, what do you recommend?"

"The cheeseburger, Grandpa. I recommend the cheeseburger."

The waiter brought their drinks and took their orders and Lucy listened to the chatter around her. Everyone was telling stories.

"Lucy, can I ask you about your mom?" Marty asked. "I've wanted to know what kind of mother she was, what her life was like over those eleven years, but I want to make sure you're OK talking about her."

"It's fine," she said. "I think she was a pretty good mom. She seemed like a normal mom, I guess. She worked for a law office, I'm not sure exactly what all she did, but she started out as a receptionist and then after a while got a job working for one of the lawyers. When I was in fourth grade she started taking classes at the local junior college. She told me she wanted to study to become a lawyer."

A surprised expression formed on Marty's face.

"Marilyn, an attorney," he said taking it in. "I didn't know she was taking classes. I never notified the school."

"Carol did," Lucy said. "She told me she called them. She said they already knew about the accident."

Lucy took a sip of her Coke.

Marty waited for her to start again.

"Her classes were on Saturday the first year, so I went with her. I was supposed to be studying in the college library, but sometimes I would just sit there watching the students come in and out. The next year, when I was in fifth grade, her class was at night, two nights a week, and she let me stay home by myself. Of course, Carol was home next door on those nights. My mom always wanted to know where I was. When I got home from school I had to call her. I talked with her the day she was in the accident, when I got home from school. I never thought about it being the last time I would talk to her."

Lucy paused trying to remember that conversation, but she couldn't.

"I think she tried her best to do things with me, but now when I think of it, I'm not sure where she found the time. We always went out together for Halloween. She loved that. She took me to Six Flags and downtown Chicago, to Navy Pier and museums. We put up a tree every Christmas, but we made our ornaments and garland out of popcorn and cranberries and cookies. Cookies were the ornaments. Then on Christmas day we started eating them and didn't take down the tree until all the cookies were gone. The first couple of days they were pretty good, but as they got older, not so good. She always got extra money at Christmas from her job. As soon as she got that check every year, she would take me out to a Christmas lunch and then drop me off at Carol's telling me she had to go talk to Santa about gifts for me. I would have a list and she would take it with her. I never saw Santa myself. She had a special bond with him and felt she could get us a better deal. Isn't that funny? That's what she used to tell me.

"She never had a boyfriend, well, that I know of. Carol was her best friend. We just lucked out that she lived next door to the house we rented. I guess she talked to Carol about things, because Carol knew about you. I didn't know about you. I try not to be mad at her for that, but . ."

Lucy didn't go on. She had tried to understand the fight between her mother and grandmother. From Lucy's perspective it seemed well out of proportion and no matter what angle she studied it from, in her mind, that conclusion never changed.

"All of that sounds like her," Marty said. "Thank you."

After lunch, Marty took Lucy to the Museum of the North. They walked through the archaeology and earth science collections and then he took her to the fine art collection. She walked through the exhibit with a different perspective than she had on her first visit here with her grandfather. She stopped and studied the different mediums and the history of Alaska depicted in each scene. She marveled at the beauty of the works and tried to see through each artist's eyes.

She watched a demonstration by an artist as he worked on a watercolor of a rainbow streaming through a mountain range and it reminded her of the one she saw on her trip through Denali National Park.

On the drive home, they were both quiet. Marty was deep in thought about what Lucy had said to him in the restaurant. He wanted to savor it. He still remembered the teen years with Marilyn and although Lucy wasn't Marilyn, Lucy would be a typical teenager starting high school. He remembered himself at that age. It was what all teenagers went through, and it was hell for the parents, or in his case, the grandparent.

Lucy was thinking about her mom. She wished her mom could see what she had accomplished. Maybe someday, her dad would.

Chapter 31

In the summer when Lucy was eight, her mom took her to Six Flags Amusement Park. She only rode on the simplest of all the roller coasters, but to Lucy the ride had seemed a cross between a bucking bronco and a drop off a cliff. Her mom had flung her arms to the heavens crying out in sheer joy as the cart seemed to fall from the sky, while Lucy had held on for dear life, knuckles turning white from the death grip on the bar. Her eyes had been shut tight.

Now as a photographer, she opened her eyes to everything. And even in those rare instances when her camera was not in her hands, her eyes would act like a shutter snapping pictures and her brain would develop the images. Why she saw things differently than most, she had no idea. Maybe it was the way her brain was wired, maybe she possessed some unique insight into things visual or maybe she saw things the way she wanted them to be not the way they actually were. But whatever the reason, it brought joy to her life. And here she was getting ready to show to anyone who cared to look how her eye portrayed the ordinary things of life as unusual, unique, exceptional.

Patty had called to set up another meeting with Lucy and Marty at the gallery. The owner and staff had chosen the pictures from Lucy's submission for exhibit and Patty wanted to review them with Lucy. In addition, Patty had made an appointment with the printer and she was taking Lucy there afterwards. Marty would get to spend the time going over the contract with Marcia White.

Patty took them to a room where a screen had been set up.

"As I go through these I'll also give you the tentative name of the photograph, but if you have a thought for a different name, let me know and we'll discuss it," Patty said switching off the light in the room. "The first three photos are the ones that I purchased from you. We're listing these as sold. It will leave you with only five prints for sale, but we feel that the sold photographs could actually bring more interest in your work."

Patty clicked a remote in her hand and the photo of the moose appeared on the screen.

"We've titled this *Haunting Eyes*. Does that seem appropriate to you Lucy?"

"It's a perfect name," Lucy said.

When the next photograph appeared on the screen, Patty said, "The bare feet in the stream we would like to title *Pink Toes*. I'll just keep on going, so stop me if you have any comments or questions. Next is the ice sculpture which we've titled *Golden Prize*. That's the end of the ones that we will be marking as sold. Now for the new ones."

The first photo that appeared on the screen was the black and white of Lily.

"Oh, remember I said that I hadn't meant to put that in the group for the art show," Lucy said. "It's a gift for Mrs. and Mrs. Amaguk."

"We want to show this one as a part of your collection Lucy," Patty said. "If you want to identify it as sold, I'll be happy to do that. It just leaves you with a very limited number of photographs that can be sold. But if that's OK with you, the gallery is fine with it. This exhibit is primarily to introduce new artists. Whether you are interested in selling your photos is really up to you. If we have enough interest in your work, we can work with you to show your work on a permanent basis in the future."

Lucy looked at her grandfather.

"It's up to you Lucy," he said. "It's your work and it's your decision."

Lucy looked at the photograph of Lily.

"It's a gift," she said.

"That's fine. We'll make it easy and title it *Lily*," Patty said.

The next picture popped up on the screen. It was the photo of Mt. McKinley sprinkled in purple and draped in a scarf of clouds.

"*Purple Majesty*," Patty said. "Next is the black and white of the suspended clouds we've titled *Hanging Clouds*."

"How about *Suspended Stratus*? We learned about clouds this year in school and you said suspended clouds when you were describing the photo."

Patty took out a pen and made a note on a pad of paper.

"Actually, I do like that better," Patty said. "We'll make the change."

On the screen the blue tree trunks appeared.

"*Truly Blue*, Patty said. "And finally *Heavenly Dance*."

The eerie black and white photo of the Northern Lights behind the grove of evergreen trees filled the screen.

"I liked your idea about combining the four photos of the Northern Lights, but I think you were right about it needing to be a really large photo and we don't have the room for it during this exhibit," Patty said. "But it's one we can look at for any future showings you may have with us. And the one of the tree stand as a textured oil painting is good too, but again we're limited to eight.

"So does this meet with your approval?"

"Yes, thank you," Lucy said. "This doesn't seem real to me."

"Well, we're about to spend some time with the printer and your grandfather's about to spend some time going over the contract," Patty said. "After that, it'll probably seem more real."

They left Marty with Marcia while Patty drove Lucy to the printers.

"I'm going to warn you," Patty said smiling at her. "Stan McMaster is not very friendly. He's all business, but he's excellent at what he does. So if he's short with you, don't take it personally."

It was hard not to take it personally. Lucy wasn't used to people like Stan McMaster. At first she was sure she didn't care for the man. But when he began preparing the prints for her review, their relationship became all about the photos and thoughts of him not being too friendly quickly left her mind. They worked well together and it didn't take long before she approved small versions of all eight photographs. Next he printed them to the correct size per Patty's direction and Lucy went back over each one to make sure they portrayed to the viewer how she saw the picture. The completed photos would go directly to the framers who Patty had already contacted, so Lucy signed and dated each one before leaving.

At the gallery Marcia was going over the contracts, printing and framing costs and the prices they were putting on the finished photos.

"Patty is picking up the cost of the printing and framing for the three originals she will be getting in place of the numbered prints she originally purchased," Marcia said.

"And I've given you the costs for the remaining five, but we've agreed to take those costs only when the photographs have been sold along with our standard commission. Based on the prices that we're placing on her pieces, she will still see a nice return. I sincerely believe that Lucy has a very promising future as a photographer, and I'm excited that she'll be a part of the exhibit this year. It's not often that we have the art work of someone as young as she is in the gallery. I'm sure you're very proud of her."

"I've watched her grow from a being lost to finding herself," Marty said. "And I'm so lucky to be a part of her journey."

"I don't get over to Spruce very often," Marcia said. "But I'll be sure to check out your bookstore the next time I'm there. Patty's mentioned it to me recently telling me it's where all the real readers go for their books."

"Well, that's really kind of her," Marty said. "The next time you're going to be in Spruce, call me and I'll give you the grand tour."

"That sounds lovely," she said. "Oh, here they are."

Patty and Lucy walked into the gallery and Marty and Marcia walked out of her office. Patty gave Lucy a hug.

"Thanks for all your help Patty," Lucy said. "If Lily were here I'd pinch her just so I'd know this is real."

Chapter 32

Marty asked Rose to help him find the appropriate dress for Lucy for the night of the gallery showing. Rose took Lucy and Lily into Fairbanks for a girl's day out. They had planned a day of shopping along with lunch at the Tea Room, a fancy place where the male population of Fairbanks was always outnumbered by a combination of ladies' clubs, girlfriend get-togethers or as in their case, girl's day out.

Lucy felt she had already tried on half the dresses in Fairbanks finding none that was perfect when they stopped for lunch. The Tea Room was decorated with starched linens and china adorned with flowers of every variety. Their table overlooked a small garden where two ladies were sitting on a bench enjoying the afternoon warmth. To Lucy it looked like they had been friends for many years. Maybe she and Lily would sit in that same spot when they were old.

For lunch they had tea served in china cups and an assortment of finger sandwiches which Lucy and Lily ate with their pinky fingers lifted high in the air. Rose tried to get them to stop, but then Lily started talking in a British accent and Lucy laughed so hard that tea came out through her nose.

"So much for acting prim and proper," Rose said.

But they were all having too much fun to really care.

"Where did you learn that accent?" Lucy asked Lily.

"It's just a little thing left over from my time as Oliver," she said raising her pinky finger again. "Of course, Oliver never drank his tea from china cups."

For dessert they were presented with an ornate glass tray of tiny cakes. It reminded Lucy of miniature versions of the first birthday cake her grandfather had bought for her. They each pointed to two and the waitress removed them from the glass tray onto small china plates sitting in front of each of them. Lucy's first one was filled with strawberry jam, the second, a creamy custard that tried to escape from the cake as she bit into it.

After lunch, they resumed the mission of finding Lucy a dress. She was back in a dressing room when Lily came running in.

"Lucy, get out here!" she yelled.

"I can't I'm half naked," Lucy said. "What's going on?"

"I saw a guy walk by on the street and he looked like the guy in the photo. You know the one on the bench."

"Did you see where he went?"

"No! I ran in here to get you. Come on!"

"Lily, I have no clothes on."

"Throw your clothes back on. Hurry!"

Lucy grabbed her pants and almost fell over trying to put them on at the speed that Lily was requesting of her. She reached for her blouse and began buttoning as quickly as her fingers would send the buttons through the corresponding hole.

"What's your mom going to say when we go flying out of here?" Lucy asked finishing with the last button.

"We'll just say we thought we saw someone we knew from school."

Finally Lucy finished getting dressed and Lily grabbed her out of the dressing room. They ran to the front door of the shop and were yanking it open as Rose yelled at them.

"Girls! Where are you going?"

"Be right back Mom," Lily said. "We thought we saw someone we knew from school."

The girls broke out onto the sidewalk, looking up and down the walkway.

"He was wearing a blue shirt," Lily said.

"I don't see anyone wearing a blue shirt," Lucy said. She looked down and notice that she had buttoned her shirt incorrectly so one side hung down longer than the other.

"Lily, you don't even know if you saw the right person," Lucy said. "I don't see anyone now and I'm standing outside on the sidewalk dressed like this."

Lily glanced over at Lucy's shirt but acted like it was buttoned normally.

"Darn, I can't believe I may have seen your dad and now he's gone," Lily said.

"Girls!" Rose yelled from the door of the store. "Please!"

Both girls walked back into the store.

"What was that all about?" asked Rose.

"I thought I saw someone from school, but I guess I didn't," Lily said. "Sorry Mom. It was just one of those spur of the moment things."

"Well, let's not have any more of those today, OK?" Rose said.

They continued from store to store looking for a dress, and Lucy was tempted to just give up and try to find something already in her closet. She glanced up at each window they passed, walking into any store that seemed promising. Just when she had lost all hope, she glanced up in the window of a small boutique at the end of the block. There on a mannequin was the perfect dress. It was a deep red with little spaghetti straps. It hung on the mannequin like the dress had been custom made just for the plastic figure.

"Look," Lucy said. "I think that's the dress."

The store clerk removed the dress from the mannequin and hung it in a dressing room for Lucy. She looked at it hanging there wishing it to fit her like it had the mannequin. She took off her blouse and slacks and then realized she had to take off her bra or it would show under the straps of the dress. She unzipped the back of the dress and slid it over her head. She couldn't get the zipper all the way up so she called for Lily.

With Lily's help, Lucy could feel the dress hugging her as the zipper progressed up her back. She turned around and looked at herself in the mirror.

"Oh my gosh, Lucy, that's beautiful, you're beautiful," Lily said. "Come out and model it for my mom."

Lucy stared at herself a moment longer and then walked out of the dressing room.

Rose looked up at her. "It's perfect," she said. "You look absolutely radiant."

Lucy grabbed for the price tag praying that it was within the budget that her grandfather had set. When she saw that it was, the grin on her face widened. She went back into the dressing room and looked at herself again in the dress. It was a picture she would never forget.

When Lucy got back home she hung the dress on the front of her closet and stared at it. Her grandfather had wanted to see it but she told him that she wanted to surprise him on the night of the exhibit.

"Don't worry," she had said. "Rose approved it."

"I wasn't worried," he had replied.

She had smiled at him, "Yes you were."

Now she picked up the dress and opened her closet door. She moved her clothes to either side down the rod and placed the dress neatly in the open space. Then she sat down on the floor and looked through her shoes. She found the little silver sandals with short heels that her grandfather had purchased for her for the dance in the seventh grade. She tried them on and they still fit her. She moved her other shoes to the side and placed the sandals directly under the red dress. Then she closed the closet door. She found a sticky note pad in her desk draw and printed KEEP OUT across the top sheet and drew a smiley face below it, tore it off the pad and stuck in on her closet door.

Chapter 33

Marty placed a sign on the front door of the Northern Lights Bookstore. Disappointing a late day shopper was not even on his mind today. Joe was closing up with him. Lucy had invited Joe personally and he had told her he wouldn't miss it for the world.

Lucy's come a long way from the first day she walked into this bookstore," Joe said. "She has you to thank for that."

"She did it all by herself," Marty said. "I was just there cheering her on."

"You may have cheered, but you did more than that," Joe said, "I know you'll never admit it."

"If I did anything for her, she did more for me," Marty said patting Joe on the back.

At home, Lucy had her cell phone tucked under her chin listening to Lily decide what she was going to wear. Lucy was only half listening to her. Lucy was so excited that her nerves were starting to play with her again. She hated it when they did that.

"So which one should I choose?" Lily asked.

"Which will you feel the best in?" Lucy asked.

"You're always answering my questions with more questions. You should be a shrink. What time do you have to be at the gallery tonight?"

"My grandpa and I have to be there at six so Marcia and Patty can get us all set up. Hopefully that will give me a little time to look at the other art work before seven."

"My mom and dad are bringing me at sevenish. That's if I can decide what to wear."

"I'm really glad you're coming Lily."

"Of course I'm coming! I wouldn't miss it for the world."

"I seem to be hearing that a lot," Lucy said mostly to herself.

Lucy was ready to go shortly after five. She could hear her grandfather pacing the floor outside her door asking her every five minutes if she was ready. Finally she opened the door and walked out of her room. Her grandfather stopped his back and forth movements and took her in.

"When did you go from ten years old to eighteen?" he asked her.

She twirled around like a model on a runway and he whistled.

"You look beautiful, honey," he said.

"Thank you Grandpa," she said.

The closer they got to Fairbanks and the gallery, the more her nerves used her body as an amusement park, sending her neurons on a wild ride. Glancing over at her, Marty recognized that look on her face and reached over to hold her hand. She didn't think it helped but decided to hold on tight just in case. Lucy hadn't been back to the gallery since she had spent the day at the printers with Patty and had no idea how her prints would looked framed, matted and hung on the gallery walls. Her mind flitted about remembering her mom, the first time she met Lily, the moose, the trip to Denali, photographic images, her grandfather. All these images came in short bursts that were replaced by the next vision, one after the other until they all left her to fend for herself.

Marty parked in a lot a block from the gallery, turned off the ignition and shifted in his seat to look at her.

"You wouldn't be here tonight if you didn't deserve it," he said trying to calm her nerves. "You mixed the unique talent you have with hard work and just look what you got Lucy."

She did look. She brought those images up again at a blinding speed to this very point in time. It was hard for her, but she closed down the amusement park and sent the neurons home. She grabbed her grandfather's hand again, but this time she smiled, big and wide like Lily had taught her. If she continued to work on it, someday it might come to her naturally.

The lights in the gallery were both bright and subdued in the exact proportion to highlight the artwork and give mystery to the space around it. Marcia greeted them, giving Lucy a hug.

"You look beautiful," Marcia said to her. "Patty's over there next to your photographs. Take your grandfather and have a look."

Lucy looked over in the direction of Patty as Patty looked up from a clipboard in her hands and waved. Lucy began the walk toward her feeling her legs become heavier with each step. She glanced from side to side taking in the art being presented by others. She wondered if she was really in this category of talent. Another hug, this time from Patty, felt like a helping hand to round up any pieces of her that wanted to scatter into the room.

"Lucy, you look lovely," Patty said pulling away from her. "Marty, nice to see you again." She stuck out her arm and he grabbed it with his right placing his left hand on top of hers and it looked to Lucy like they were beginning to play some childhood game.

"Well, what do you think?" Patty asked sweeping her arm in the direction of Lucy's photographs.

Lucy took one step back and then another. Her eyes slowly progressed over each photograph hanging there, perfectly matted and framed, the light reflecting in such a way as to not cast shadows on the glass. She had to remind herself that she had taken these photographs, that they represented her eyes, the way she saw the world. She wished Lily was here to pinch.

"Patty, Lucy's work is beautifully presented," Marty finally said. "Don't you agree Lucy?"

Lucy turned and stared at him and then at Patty.

"I don't know what to say," she said. "You turned my photos into works of art."

"Hardly," Patty said. "Your photographs are the works of art, we just accessorized them, like you in that striking dress."

That didn't make sense to Lucy. She was sure that this dress made her look pretty, without it, she would be like a simple photograph. But she smiled at Patty anyway.

"You have some time to look around if you'd like," Patty said watching Lucy closely. She wondered if Lucy really had no idea how beautiful she was. Patty still failed to see Marilyn in her. Sure, occasionally when Lucy smiled or made some type of gesture, she would see Marilyn for the briefest of moments.

"I'd love that," Lucy said. "Grandpa?"

"Go ahead," he said wanting her to experience this on her own.

She looked at him trying to decide why he was sending her on her own, like she was about to learn some lesson. But finally she shrugged her shoulders and walked away from him, from Patty and from her photographs hanging so perfectly on the gallery wall.

She took in works created in watercolors, oils and fabrics and pieces carved, sculpted and welded. She stopped to read the artists' profiles. She wondered if there was a profile of her next to her photographs. She hadn't remembered seeing it. Lucy was reading the profile of an artist who worked with metals when she turned around and came face to face with the artist.

"I'm Nancy Carter," she said holding out her hand.

"Lucy, Lucy Wright," Lucy said taking her hand and feeling Nancy's firm grip. "I like your work."

"Thanks," she said. "Are you an artist?"

Lucy had never thought of herself as an artist, just a photographer. "I have photographs over there." She pointed in the direction of the wall where her pieces hung.

"I saw those earlier," Nancy said. "I never imaged that you would be so young. What are you, eighteen?"

Lucy looked down at her silver sandals. "Fourteen," she said.

Nancy took a step back and looked at her. "OK, now I'm really impressed."

Lucy didn't know what to say to her.

"Well, I suppose you're walking around the show before it opens," Nancy said saving her from having to reply. "It's been nice to meet you Lucy."

"It's nice to meet you," Lucy said walking on to the next exhibitor.

Lucy wondered through each exhibitor's work meeting an oil painter and a man who worked with junk he found alongside the road, welding the pieces into identifiable figures. Finished, she looked down at her watch and saw that it was nearly seven so she headed back to her photography. There she saw the profile that the gallery had written about her and she read it in a whisper to herself.

At the age of fourteen, Lucy Wright is the youngest artist to be included in the Alaska Artists exhibit held each year at the Reston-White Fine Art Gallery. Her photography has been seen in local publications and her talent has been spotlighted on The Today Show *in New York. Originally from Illinois, Lucy became an Alaskan four years ago finding a love of photography at the same time. Through her photography she embodies the spirit and beauty of Alaska. She sees things in her subjects that most people miss and develops her photos, whether in color or black and white, to show what we might have otherwise failed to see.*

The Amaguks were greeted by Marcia. "Ben," she said taking his hand. "It's an honor to have you here this evening."

"We're happy to be here," he said. "Please let me introduce you to my wife and daughter." But Lily had already spotted Lucy and had taken off through the crowd that had started to gather at the gallery.

"Lucy!" she yelled giving her best friend a hug. When she broke away she looked up at the photo that Lucy had taken of her. She backed away to get a better look. Lucy watched as Lily's parents left Marcia and headed toward her. Lily still hadn't said anything, instead appearing to study her portrait, her lips parted but no words emerging, an abnormal occasion for Lily. Rose walked up to Lucy and gave her a hug and then looked at her daughter following her gaze up to the photograph. "Oh, my," she said.

"It's a gift for you," Lucy said to Mrs. Amaguk. "You and Mr. Amaguk, for everything you've done for me."

For the first time since Lucy had met them, no one in the Amaguk family seemed to be able to say a word. Lucy watched a tear fall from Mrs. Amaguk's eye and began to worry that something was wrong. Then Lily's mom turned to Lucy and hugged her so tight Lucy thought she would never again lose parts of herself to the outside world.

Marty watched the exchange from across the room. It tore at his heart, this happiness he carried inside him.

As the guest arrived, Marcia greeted them all with the flair of a gallery owner.

"Jack!" she exclaimed. "You made it."

"Of course, I wouldn't miss it for the world," he said. "If it wasn't for you, I would be living a different life now."

"I'm sure your artwork would have taken you to the same place. But speaking of a different life, how's life in the tropics? Don't you miss us here in Alaska?"

"I miss Alaska, but I've found I'm a warm blooded animal," he laughed. "I'm still waiting for you to come see my workshop. I think you'd really appreciate it in January or February."

"I may just take you up on that one of these days. In the meantime, enjoy the show and I'll talk with you later."

He left her and Marcia greeted the next guests walking in the front door of the gallery.

As guests entered the gallery, they moved through the displays taking in the works of the new artists. A couple holding hands entered Lucy's area and stopped in front of her photograph of the moose.

"I better leave you to your fans," Lily said. "I'll walk around and see you later. Which one is Patty?"

Lucy looked around her and spotted Patty on the other side of the gallery. "Over there in the black dress."

Now other people were stopping to read her profile and look at her photographs. And they were complimenting her on her work. She watched some back up to what seemed a specific spot on the floor to better observe her photographs. She saw her grandfather standing off to the side watching her and she waved at him. He smiled back at her. A smile that said so many things to Lucy that she wished she had her camera with her to capture it.

Lucy felt incredibly happy. She thought about how extraordinary her life was, how remarkable it had become. And for the first time in her life she felt content. It was an odd feeling for her, a sensation she'd never experienced before. One she wished she could photograph.

She brought her mind back to the room and watched a man study her photographs.

"You have a very remarkable way of seeing things," he said. "Have you studied photography or are you just naturally this talented?"

"I've taken a couple of classes," Lucy said. "Are you an artist?"

"Well, some people say I am," he laughed. "Marcia actually gave me my start right here in this gallery. It was a lucky break for me, otherwise I would probably still be just teaching art instead of creating it."

He was tall and Lucy had to actually look up to talk to him. That didn't happen very often to her. She was still one of the tallest girls in school, even in high school. It felt nice to look up instead of down for a change.

From across the room, Lily was introducing herself to Patty pointing over at Lucy. She stopped and dropped her arm to her side staring at the man talking to Lucy.

"Who's that man talking to Lucy?" Lily asked.

"What man?" Patty asked, looking through the crowded gallery toward Lucy.

"Did Lucy show you a picture of a guy on the bench that she found in a box of her mother's things?"

"No, I don't think so."

Lily pointed to the man talking to Lucy, and Patty caught a glimpse of him through the crowd.

"That's Jack Davis," Patty said. "He's one of the gallery's previous new artists. Marcia invited him in celebration of Alaska's 50th anniversary. She invited all the past artists.

"Why would Lucy's mom have a photograph of him?" Lily asked.

"Are you sure that's the guy in the photo?" Patty asked.

"Pretty sure," Lily said. "I think I also saw him when we were shopping in Fairbanks."

"He doesn't live in Fairbanks," Patty said. "I'm sure you're confusing him with someone else."

"By the way, I'm Jack Davis," he said.

"Lucy Wright," she said taking his hand and shaking it. "It's nice to meet you."

"Wright?" he said as if trying to recall a memory. "I used to know a Wright."

Someone tapped Lucy on the shoulder and she turned around. "I'm from the *Fairbanks News*," the woman said extending her hand. "May I take a picture of you next to your photographs?"

This time Lucy pinched herself as she moved next to one of her photographs, the one entitled *Golden Prize*. That's exactly how this remarkable moment felt to her. Like an incredible golden prize. Lucy smiled and watched the camera's flash fill the room with the same warm light that filled her from the top of her head down to her shocking pink toes.

Author's Notes

Much of this story came purely from photographs which, of course, were how Lucy saw Alaska. Please forgive me for any mistakes I made about Alaska or its people. This is only how Lucy, with her eye for observing things in a special way, saw them in the story.

Spruce, Alaska, is a fictitious place. While places like Denali National Park and Fairbanks are real, the characters, incidents and places within Fairbanks that occur in the story are fabricated. Some of the places within the boundary of Denali National Park are real; however, I took great liberty in imaging what Lucy observed and experienced (or in other words, I made them up). Elm, Illinois, is also a fictitious place. New York, Matt Lauer and *The Today Show* do exist, but again the places within New York, events and other people that Lucy experiences there are fabricated. If Matt Lauer was interviewing someone like Lucy, I have no idea what questions he would have asked her. I as the writer got to ask the questions that Lucy wasn't expecting.

All of us, including Lucy, take our dreams and failures, our joys and sorrows and we take the people we love and move forward through time. This is how Lucy pictures it. And I'm just telling her stories.

Special thanks to those who read this book and offered constructive advice including my husband Bob, Susan Mincey, Terri Sutton, Cindi Riekena, and most of all Norma Busch.